HOME TO TEXAS

Center Point
Large Print

Also by Max McCoy and available from Center Point Large Print:

The Sixth Rider
Sons of Fire
The Wild Rider

**This Large Print Book carries the
Seal of Approval of N.A.V.H.**

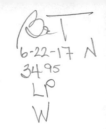
HOME TO TEXAS

Max McCoy

CENTER POINT LARGE PRINT
THORNDIKE, MAINE

This Center Point Large Print edition is published in
the year 2017 by arrangement with the author.

Copyright © 1995 by Max McCoy.

The text of this Large Print edition is unabridged.
In other aspects, this book may vary
from the original edition.
Printed in the United States of America
on permanent paper.
Set in 16-point Times New Roman type.

ISBN: 978-1-68324-383-0

Library of Congress Cataloging-in-Publication Data

Names: McCoy, Max, author.
Title: Home to Texas / Max McCoy.
Description: Center Point Large Print edition. | Thorndike, Maine :
Center Point Large Print, 2017.
Identifiers: LCCN 2017005650 | ISBN 9781683243830
    (hardcover : alk. paper)
Subjects: LCSH: Large type books. | GSAFD: Western stories.
Classification: LCC PS3563.C3523 H66 2017 | DDC 813/.54—dc23
LC record available at https://lccn.loc.gov/2017005650

For my mother,
Mary Carter McCoy
1927–1986

Author's Note

As with *Sons of Fire*, much of what follows is true. Although the Fenns of Missouri are a product of the imagination, the migration of families during the Civil War from the bloody Missouri–Kansas border to the comparative safety of Texas is fact. Any errors in interpretation, however, are mine alone.

I am indebted to a number of individuals who were willing to share their time and their knowledge of the period. Chief among them is Arnold Schofield, historian at Fort Scott National Historic Site. Jan and Roger O'Connor also deserve special thanks for their help in locating research material. Recognition is also long overdue to my good friend Allen "Bud" Jones, a remarkable man who was born out of time. Finally, I would like to thank librarians everywhere, without whom works like this would not be possible.

—Max McCoy
Pittsburg, Kansas
March 1995

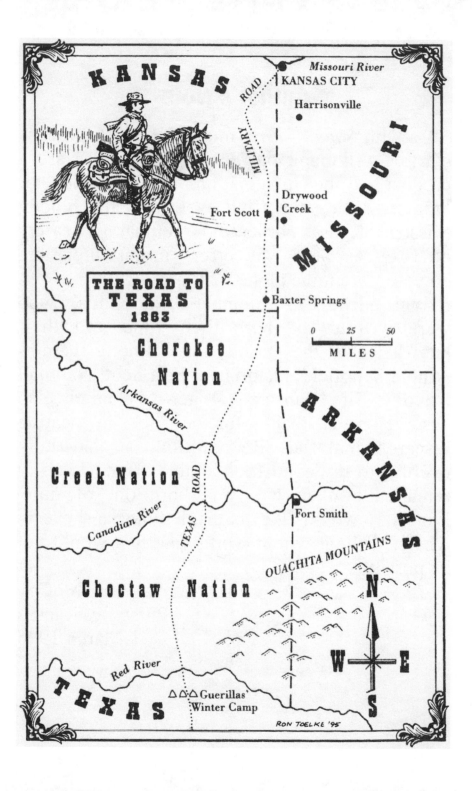

KANSAS

Missouri River
KANSAS CITY

Harrisonville

MILITARY ROAD

Drywood
Creek

Fort Scott

MISSOURI

THE ROAD TO
TEXAS
1863

Baxter Springs

Cherokee
Nation

0   25   50
MILES

Arkansas River

ARKANSAS

Creek Nation

Canadian River

TEXAS ROAD

Fort Smith

OUACHITA MOUNTAINS

Choctaw   Nation

N

Red River

△△△ Guerillas'
Winter Camp

W   E

TEXAS

S

RON TOELKE '95

Prologue

May 1863

Long before Thomas Moonlight reached the Osage village, he could hear, above the howling of the dogs and the rush of the night wind in the trees, the lamentations of the women. It was an unearthly sound, he thought, one that defied the human vocal range. The chant was punctuated at regular intervals by uncontrolled sobbing.

"Listen," Moonlight said. "They must have lost some of their own in the fight."

Major Doudna drew his horse alongside Moonlight's.

The column of soldiers behind them came to a disjointed stop.

The keening had reached a previously unknown octave. It filled Moonlight's soul with fear and wonder, and he was at once afraid that it would continue and fearful that it would stop.

"It is chilling," Doudna said. He pulled a flask from his coat, took a long swallow, then offered the whiskey to Moonlight.

Moonlight drank sparingly.

"Their squaws make the racket," Doudna said. "It is the sound of an animal in pain. It is in these ungodly rituals that they reveal themselves as

9

little better than the beasts of the field. This, Captain, is what we have to deal with."

"And yet," Moonlight said, "there is something heart-wrenchingly human in the sound. I have the distinct feeling, Major, that we are listening to our prehistoric ancestors petitioning the universe for mercy."

Moonlight handed back the flask.

"Perhaps," Doudna said.

Doudna returned the whiskey to his pocket and turned the collar of his coat against the cool night air, all the while shaking his head.

Bone Heart was troubled.

He sat on his heels in the middle of the Osage village, watching in respectful silence as the women of the slain warriors chanted the Death Song. The warriors had been painted for burial, their limbs coaxed into the sitting position of a baby within its mother's belly, and each had been lashed with his back to the trunk of a tree. Their women knelt before the bodies, their coarse black hair brushing the ground, the right sides of their faces daubed with the blue earth of mourning.

It had been a long while since the Osage had sent dead warriors upon the sacred path.

The face of Night-Has-Returned, Bone Heart's brother, was drawn tight in death. He had been the first to fall, killed without respect by an offhand pistol shot when ten warriors had attempted a parley with twenty-two horse soldiers crossing Osage land. The strange soldiers had refused to identify themselves, had ignored a request to accompany them to the bluecoat fort at Humboldt. The leader of the horse soldiers, a huge man with a bald head and a flowing gray beard, had sharp words for the soldier who had fired the killing shot—but he had no words for the Osage. The strange soldiers had ridden on.

The warriors returned to the village with the body of Night-Has-Returned across the saddle of his pony. Soon Chief Hard Rope was leading two hundred Osage warriors, including Bone Heart, after the strangers. They chased the soldiers across the prairie, trading shots, and two strangers and another warrior fell dead from their horses. But in time, the Osage had the soldiers in a trap, forcing them to abandon their horses and make a last stand upon a sandy island in the middle of the muddy Verdigris River. Eventually the soldiers ran out of powder and shot, and fought their last desperate struggle with fists and knives and the butts of their guns.

The strange soldiers had been rubbed out.

Bone Heart himself had killed the leader of the strange soldiers. The big man had fought bravely. There had been no fear of death in his eyes, even as Bone Heart had driven his knife deep into the strange chief's stomach. The other warriors had taken scalp locks from their soldiers, but Bone

Heart had returned to the village with something finer dangling from *his* coup stick: the soldier chief's great gray beard.

It had been a magnificent fight, and Bone Heart had avenged well his brother's death. But the source of Bone Heart's unease lay in the papers, now smeared with bloody fingerprints, that the warriors had taken from the soldier chief and the other strangers. No one in the village could read, and without knowing what talk the papers commanded, there was no way to be certain of which side the strange soldiers belonged. It would be very bad if the papers said the strangers were friends of the bluecoats.

Bone Heart heard the sound of shod horses approaching the village, and he scooped up the bloody papers and hid them in the brush. When one of the leaders of the bluecoats—a strange pale man who had a good Indian name, that of the light of the full moon—had demanded to see what they had taken from the strange soldiers, Bone Heart had lied. He said there had been nothing to take. But then he became afraid that somehow, in the strange way of the whites, the papers were already singing out from their hiding place.

Bone Heart had retrieved the bloody mess and given it to Moonlight.

After studying the papers for a moment, the bluecoat leader grinned.

"Congratulations," he told Bone Heart and the

others. "You have killed a demon by the name of Charlie Harrison, a great bearded chief and enemy of the Union. You have much to celebrate."

Bone Heart was filled with pride.

Later, when Moonlight asked Bone Heart if he would help to hunt down other enemies of the bluecoats—men like Quantrill, of which Bone Heart had heard much—and those who sided with the Cherokee, who were a nation of liars whom the Osage hated, Bone Heart had agreed and painted himself for battle.

The Osage had become a nation of warriors once more.

1

October 1863

Something's out there."

Joshua Tobias cocked both of the navy revolvers as he drew them from his belt. He nudged the door of the abandoned barn with his shoulder, and the dry leather hinges creaked, opening just enough for him to peer outside.

The moon was new and cast no light, and with the exception of the outline of a partially toppled chimney that marked the spot where a house once stood, the landscape was a dark smudge beneath a canopy of hard bright stars. The night was still, but he could hear no trace of the sound that had inspired his fear—the irregular rasp of something moving cautiously through the hard winter stubble.

Nearby, an owl called.

Far across the barren fields, another owl joined the first in asking the infernal question. Joshua glared at the darkness, daring whatever was out there to show itself.

"I can't see a thing," he said softly, his breath billowing in the cold and frosting his beard. "But I know somethin's out there. It's been following us, John, for three days. I've had a bad feeling ever since we busted caps on that sorry excuse for a dirt farmer."

John Tobias was stretched out on the straw, fully clothed, with his black slouch hat covering his eyes. The hat—which was his only article of clothing not splattered with red Missouri mud—was badly beaten, but the brim was pinned in front, and a turkey feather was set at a rakish angle on the left side. His hands were folded over the butt of a meticulously clean and loaded .44-caliber revolver.

Beside his cousin, beneath a ragged and lice-infested blanket, was a woman.

"Shut the door," John said from beneath the hat. "It's cold."

Joshua carefully eased the hammers down on powder-darkened nipples topped by bright percussion caps and returned the revolvers to his belt. "Maybe we should saddle up," he suggested as he pulled the door shut and set the latch. "Truth to tell, I'd rest easier someplace else. Down by the river, maybe."

In the center of the dirt floor was a lamp improvised from a tin cup of rancid bacon fat, with a rag for a wick. The motion of the closing door caused the flame to undulate and cast grotesque shadows on the rough-hewn walls.

Joshua sat cross-legged in front of the light. He picked the cleanest piece of straw he could find within arm's reach and stuck it in the corner of his mouth.

"You'd rest fine here," John said, "if only you'd quit worrying so. Let it go. There's nobody out there. Hell, the Dutch make so much noise they couldn't sneak up on our poor deaf grandmother, and she's been dead for three years."

"Maybe it ain't the Dutch," Joshua said.

John removed his hat.

"I've never known you to be afraid of the Yankees before," he said. "What the hell has gotten into you now?"

"This is something different."

"How?"

Joshua shrugged and thoughtfully chewed the straw.

The woman beside his cousin roused and propped herself up on an elbow. The blanket fell away, revealing a swollen breast with a drop of milk gleaming from the tip of a bruised nipple. The woman brushed a tangle of dark hair from her eyes and mumbled a man's name, as if expecting an answer.

"Puddin', go back to sleep," John said, replacing the blanket. "Everything's all right."

As the woman groaned and lay back down Joshua struggled to put into words how close to the animals they had been rendered by the war, how all of their finer emotions had been eclipsed by instinct. Bravery and cowardice were just words; you fought when you had to and ran when you could. There was neither modesty nor shame now, only the alternating fear of death and the thrill of having survived by making others die.

"Rabbits and wolves," he said finally.

"What nonsense are you talking now?" his cousin asked, but Joshua couldn't explain it. "You've got yourself good and spooked. Give it up and get some rest. We have to move at first light if we're going to meet up with the boys in the Indian Nations, and I don't want you sleeping in the saddle."

Joshua made a face and spat out the straw.

"We shouldn't have shot the farmer," he said. "I haven't felt bad about anything else we've done, because we done what we had to do, and it was all good and milit'ry. But the farmer was different. He might have been a Yankee sympathizer, but we couldn't prove it. . . . John, what if we shot an innocent man?"

"Joshua," his cousin said wearily, "there's no such thing."

Joshua sighed. His cousin was the elder by two years, and was usually right about things, but his reassurances did little to ease the knot in Joshua's stomach. Joshua blew out the light, and watched as the red ember of the wick struggled against the darkness and lost. Then he reclined, adjusted the straw beneath his head, and closed his eyes. He silently mouthed the words of a childhood prayer. His right palm was touching the butt of one of the navies, and his index finger rested reassuringly on the cold brass of the trigger guard.

A soft, wet sucking sound brought Joshua Tobias awake. His eyes snapped open and he lay still for a moment, staring up at a sliver of stars that were visible through a crack in the barn's roof. His heart began to pound like a locomotive.

"John?" he whispered.

There was no reply save for the peculiar coppery smell of fresh blood. He came to his knees, cocked the revolver in his right hand, and swung it wildly in the darkness.

"John?" he shrieked.

With his left hand he dug into the breast pocket of his coat, found a match, and struck it with his thumb. The match sputtered and flared, and a piece of the burning head came off under his nail.

He dropped the match.

It took a moment for his brain to register what his eyes had seen in the brief blue flare of the match: a grinning Indian, with greased hair and painted face, holding a hand over his cousin's mouth while blood surged from a slit beneath his cousin's chin. In the Indian's hand was a curved skinning knife. His cousin's eyes were wide and pleading as rose-colored bubbles bloomed from his neck.

Before the match hit the ground, and just as his finger began to tighten on the trigger, Joshua found himself driven forward as if kicked by a mule. His revolver spat its ball harmlessly into the roof. He landed on his face in the dirt and dried manure of the barn floor, his ears ringing, a peculiar warmth spreading across his back.

Someone lit the tin cup of bacon grease.

The barn was filled with the smoke and the sulfurous stench of black powder. The navy had fallen half a yard away, and Joshua's fingers groped for it. A boot came down upon his hand, but Joshua didn't have the strength to cry out.

"Where is Quantrill?"

With the boot still firmly in place, Captain Thomas Moonlight knelt. He had a long tanned face that made his blue eyes seem even paler, and a finely trimmed mustache that resembled

18

corn silk. He removed his hat, then pulled off his gloves.

"How old are you, son?" he asked.

"Eighteen," Joshua managed.

"Damned young to die," the captain said evenly. "But you've taken a pistol ball square in the spine. Can you move your legs? No, I reckoned not."

Joshua turned his head toward his cousin, who now appeared quite dead. The Indian was at work with the skinning knife, laying bare the white bone beneath the scalp. The woman was huddled against the wall, the blanket pulled tightly over her head.

"Quite a savage, isn't he?" Moonlight asked. "But a brother, nonetheless. 'For he today that sheds his blood with me shall be my brother; be he ne'er so vile, this day shall gentle his condition.'"

There was a wet sliding sound that reminded Joshua of skinning rabbits as the Indian pulled his cousin's scalp free of the skull. Joshua choked back a column of bile that rose volcanically in his throat.

"Now," Moonlight said. "If you don't want Bone Heart to lift your hair also, you'll tell me where that devil Quantrill is and what he's up to. Hurry, for you don't have much time left."

Joshua swallowed and closed his eyes.

"Bound for Texas."

"Where is he now?"

"Don't know," Joshua said, and licked his lips.

19

"The boys scattered after the fight at Baxter Springs. The colonel told us to rendezvous in the Nations and beat a path down the Texas Road to the Red River."

Moonlight frowned.

"I could guess that much," he said. "I want to know where Quantrill is *now.*"

"I have no idea where the colonel might be."

"He doesn't deserve the title," Moonlight said. "My tracker Bone Heart has more basic decency than the infamous Quantrill. At least the Osage religion condones the murder, rape, and robbery of one's enemies."

Joshua's eyes narrowed with guilt.

"Who's the woman?" Moonlight asked. "One of Quantrill's whores?"

"Ain't no whore," Joshua said. "Found her in the woods, half-crazy and crying about her dead kid. Never could get a name out of her. We was going to leave her with the first family we came to, but we never found none. Everybody's gone."

Joshua began to cough.

"I'll see that she's taken care of," Moonlight said.

"Yankees seem to have a peculiar way of taking care of people," Joshua said, and smiled. Blood etched the spaces between his teeth.

Moonlight drew the .44-caliber Remington revolver from its holster for the second time that night. He laid the muzzle squarely against the back of Joshua's head, which was turned to face his dead cousin.

"'Go thou,'" Moonlight said as he squeezed the trigger, "'and fill another room in hell.'"

2

The sun was a tarnished disk behind a blanket of scalloped clouds on the western horizon, casting a weak light that robbed the prairie of its color. Shadows pooled, and spread like the rising of an inland sea, a relentless tide of muted blues and grays that blotted up the terrain.

Speed, thought Frank Fenn. *We need to cover more ground, to make up for lost time, to put as much distance between us and this godforsaken country as we can before nightfall.*

Even the air seemed dead to the concerns of men. There was no wind, and sounds were curiously muffled in the unnatural stillness. Conversation became a sleep-inducing drone, and distant gunshots were but the popping of trees in winter.

It seems as if we're crawling, but I dare not push the team harder. Caitlin has complained about our reckless pace, but the longer we remain here the more certain it is we'll stumble upon a Union patrol.

The little Rucker ambulance wagon, with its

green sides and bright red wheels, seemed to be the only bit of life on the soundless and mono-chromatic landscape. It bounced and clattered over the prairie, the USA that was proclaimed in bold black letters on its canopied sides shook, and its hubs howled for grease.

Two men, three women, a child, and an infant, Frank thought. *Seven human beings in search of refuge.*

The unruly team that pulled the wagon often attempted to go in two directions at once, snapped at one another with bared teeth, and left steaming piles of horse apples that marked the trail.

Patrick Fenn rode ahead of the wagon, his collar turned against the October chill, his coat hiding a mismatched pair of revolvers in his belt. Although his eyes stung, he remained alert, always scanning the terrain one hundred yards ahead.

For hours they had passed nothing but blackened chimneys that stood like unlettered monuments to the war that had devastated the border between the older slaveholding state of Missouri and the new free-soil state of Kansas. Their flight from Cass County had been unchecked; the border had become a sort of purgatory on earth, devoid of fences or domesticated animals or human beings in residence.

The family carried everything they owned in a two-wheeled cart: a few pots and pans, a couple of old chairs, a wooden box filled with knives and forks, and whatever else they managed to salvage from the ashes of their home.

The cart was pulled by the husband. He walked with a limp, and bloodstained rags were wrapped around what was left of his shoes. His cheeks were hollow and his eyes blazed in their sockets.

The mother wore a soiled, faded dress and carried an infant wrapped in a dirty blanket in her arms. A few steps behind her walked a young boy in equally ragged clothes. His dark hair was long and stringy, and rivulets of snot ran from his nostrils. Every few seconds he coughed and wiped his nose with a greasy sleeve.

The husband put down the cart and waited for the approach of the ambulance wagon, watching from the corners of his bloodshot eyes.

Frank kept the team at a steady pace. He did not want to steer around them, because that would have been a bald-faced insult, but he did not want to stop, either. When the father saw that the team was not going to slow, he sprang up and grasped the bridle of the nearest horse.

"Whoa," the man said.

"Let go of the team," Frank said.

"Hold on, neighbor," the man said. "We're in a desperate situation here."

"We can't help you," Frank said.

"All we need is a little food," the woman said in a voice that was close to tears.

"We don't have any," Caitlin said. The family

made her uneasy, and she instinctively held Annabel a little more tightly in her arms.

"Pardon me," the man said, "but that's hard to believe, considering the fine wagon you've got."

"She speaks the truth," Frank said. "Stay clear."

"Then you could at least let us ride for a spell," the man said, still holding tightly to the bridle of the shuffling horse. "We can't go on much further. Look at my feet. They've been bleeding since yesterday."

"I'm sorry, but there's no room. You'll have to make do."

The boy had left his mother's side and had reappeared at the front wheel, by Caitlin. He scrambled up the wheel and peered intently at her and the baby, and a wave of revulsion gripped Caitlin.

Not only was the boy dirty and sick, but the corners of his eyes were filled with yellow pus and bugs crawled in his hair. The boy alarmed Caitlin—his unclean appearance touched some animal fear deep within her gut—and she wanted to push him to the ground, to get as far away as possible. Oblivious of his effect on her, the boy leaned so close to Caitlin that the sickly-sweet stench of infection made her shut her eyes and turn her head.

"Get back," she said.

"I'm hungry."

She felt guilty for harboring such animosity toward a child, but she could not help herself.

The boy coughed, spraying Caitlin and the baby, wiped his nose with his sleeve, and dropped down.

"You had best let go of the team," Frank said.

The man refused.

"Please, help us," the woman pleaded. "We'll die out here on the prairie. It would be the same as murder, you leaving us out here. Can't you see the boy's sick and we're starving?"

Frank took up the whip.

"You would beat me like an animal?" the man asked.

Frank brought the whip down sharply across his shoulders. The man yelped and let go of the team, and Frank snapped the reins. The wagon jerked forward.

"Damn you," the man said as the wagon passed by. "If only I had a gun, things would be different."

"You're right," Patrick said from atop Raven. "You'd be dead."

Patrick held a hand in the air and motioned for the ambulance to lessen the pace. The ground had become flinty, and his horse had already stumbled twice, its iron shoes sparking.

It would be quicker if we crossed into the Kansas side, but we would be sure to encounter

25

some unpleasant business along the military road. No, better to continue down the Missouri side, then cut the corner into the Nations.

Frank Fenn felt the axle break as one of the front wheels came up hard against a boulder hidden by a clump of dead grass, and Patrick turned his horse in time to see the iron-rimmed wheel snap free of the linchpin and bounce away. The front corner of the ambulance tilted earthward, spilling his sister Caitlin and her Bible onto the ground.

Frank Fenn rode the dashboard like a sailor fighting a heavy sea as the broken axle dug into the earth, cocking the front wheel at an awkward angle that threatened to overturn the little wagon. Frank stood upon the brake. He wrapped the reins around both fists and put his back against the team, but the confused horses continued to struggle against the unnatural drag behind them. The rear wheel opposite the broken axle began to lift.

Patrick jumped from the saddle, stumbled for a few steps, then rushed to the team. He grabbed the bridle of the nearest horse and planted his feet. His boots skidded over the cold ground, and he watched the rear wheel as it spun lazily above the ground. The horses stopped and then shuffled backward a bit, and the ambulance came to rest, rocking heavily on its springs.

Frank sighed with relief, then slid to the ground and began to unhitch the team.

The wail of a child erupted from inside the wagon, causing Frank's heart to sink to his stomach. He struggled for the breath to speak.

"Who's hurt?" he called.

"Little Frank's got a bump on his head the size of a walnut," said Patrick, who had already lifted the canvas and was taking a quick census. "Jenny's got a scratch on her forehead. Trudy was holding Annabel, and they both seem fit enough."

Patrick retrieved the big Bible from the ground and helped Caitlin up. She hopped unsteadily to the wagon and glared at Frank. "I've only got one leg left," she said, shaking with anger. "Do you think I want to snap it off and spend the rest of my life scooting along the ground like some kind of two-legged dog?"

Tight-lipped, Frank jumped down and looked ruefully at their sister.

"All this family has left in the world is each other and this sorry Yankee idea of a wagon," Caitlin went on. "If Pa were alive, he'd knock some sense into your head. I reckon you learned to drive a team from one of those books you read back east. Did you learn how to fix axles, too?"

"It was an accident," Jenny said protectively as she climbed down from the wagon, Little Frank on her hip. "Let's not start blaming each other for things. It's done, and the question now is how to fix things."

"The axle's busted clean in two," Patrick said,

squatting for a better look. "We're going to need a good-sized piece of timber to replace it, at least as thick as your leg."

"Where's the closest stand of wood?" Caitlin asked.

"Drywood Creek, most likely," Patrick said. "Three or four miles to the south. I reckon it will take the rest of the day to find the right tree, hack our piece out, and bring it back."

"Then how long will it take to fix?"

Patrick withdrew an ax from the back of the ambulance.

"Another day at least," he said, testing the blade of his ax with his thumb. "And that's reckoning that the wheel can be straightened enough to use. You might as well make camp here as best you can."

"Two days," Frank said. "In two days we could have been in the Indian Nations."

"Then we'll be there in four," Patrick said.

"Give me the ax," Frank said. "I'll go for the timber."

"Frank, you'd better stay with the wagon," Patrick said as he swung up in the saddle. "I'm sure you can do this as quick as I can, but I reckon Jenny would just feel better having you here."

"We'll need some food," Frank said. "All the farms have been picked clean for miles around, but we might be lucky enough to find a squirrel or a rabbit that somebody else missed."

Patrick pulled his one good revolver from beneath his coat and handed it to the Indian girl. It was a Colt, .36 caliber, with a fully capped and loaded cylinder. The one he kept in his belt was a Joslyn that could carry only four rounds, since two of the chambers were cracked.

"Let Trudy hunt," he said.

Trudy nodded and took the gun.

"Well," Caitlin said, retrieving her crutches from the bed of the ambulance. "That's the plan. The rest of us should start gathering whatever we can find that will burn. It's going to be cold tonight, and judging from those clouds on the horizon, we're going to have an early snow."

Patrick self-consciously gave Trudy a smile and winked at his sister. Then he walked his horse a few yards away from the others and motioned for a word with his older brother. Frank held the bridle while Patrick spoke softly enough that the others couldn't hear.

"If I'm not back tomorrow, mount them double on the team and get them out of here," Patrick said. "This is a dismal place—you'll freeze or starve to death if a Yankee patrol doesn't catch you first. They need you with them . . ."

Frank Fenn finished the sentence in his mind: *. . . and not swinging at the end of a rope.*

3

Snowflakes swirled out of the darkness as Thomas Moonlight dismounted at the field headquarters of General James G. Blunt, Union commander of the District of the Frontier. Moonlight handed the reins to one of Blunt's troopers and ordered him to treat Cerberus as gently as a rich widow.

Moonlight paused at the entrance to Blunt's tent and smoothed his hair and mustache before announcing himself. Then one of the general's senior bodyguards parted the flap and escorted Moonlight inside.

Blunt was seated at his field desk. He looked up from his reports and studied Moonlight, then asked the sergeant to leave them. The general was a short man with dark hair and a swarthy complexion, and he seemed self-conscious in front of this blond giant. Blunt lit a cigar, then offered one to Moonlight, who refused.

"Report," Blunt said, smoke curling from the corners of his mouth. Moonlight withdrew a sheaf of bloodstained papers and placed them on the general's desk.

"Loyalty oaths, sir," Moonlight said. "Some of the partisans had two or three on them, each swearing allegiance to the Union. Those account for thirteen of Quantrill's men."

Blunt poured a snifter of brandy from a bottle on his desk, then took a long drink, as if girding himself for the next question.

"What of Quantrill?" he asked.

"In hiding," Moonlight said. "Waiting to rendez-vous in the Nations and lead his men to the Red River. He will soon be out of our reach."

"Damn him," Blunt said, rubbing his jaw. "The fool thought he'd killed me at Baxter Springs. If he'd left any prisoners alive, he would have learned that they'd killed Major Curtis instead."

Two weeks earlier—October 6, 1863—Quantrill had chanced upon a wagon train composed of Blunt and a hundred of his men just outside of Baxter Springs, Kansas, above the Indian Nations. Blunt had mistaken Quantrill's line of ambiguously clad raiders for an honor guard sent to greet him from the Union outpost at Baxter Springs, and the mistake had nearly proved fatal. In addition to killing seventy-nine of Blunt's men, the guerrilla chieftain also captured all of the general's correspondence, his commissions, two stands of colors, and the general's own sword. Blunt himself had only narrowly escaped capture by running wildly in fear of his life.

"Begging the general's pardon," Moonlight said as the general appeared lost in thoughts of

31

his own. Moonlight poured himself a shot of the brandy. "I await your orders, sir."

"Orders?" Blunt asked. "I want Quantrill. I want him to pay for the murder of my men . . . and of my reputation."

Moonlight smiled knowingly.

"Until I have Quantrill," Blunt continued, "I want you to hunt down as many of the men who participated in the burning of Lawrence and in the massacre at Baxter Springs as you can. No quarter, Captain."

"'Cry havoc,'" Moonlight recited, "'and let slip the dogs of war.'"

"Your tactics have worked well thus far," Blunt said admiringly. "That red Indian of yours—bless his murderous soul—has proved more effective at bringing these traitors to task than anyone expected."

"Thank you, sir," Moonlight said. "It *is* a different war here on the frontier. One has to think—and to fight—differently in order to be successful."

"You are correct about fighting differently, of course," the general said. "Tell me, Captain, what besides their intimate knowledge of the country and their secret network of support make the guerrillas most effective?"

"Their hatred of us," Moonlight said. "Their uncommon courage. Horsemanship. And, of course, the fact that we have placed them in a position of fighting to the death."

"No, no," Blunt said, waving Moonlight's comments aside. "Think in terms of firepower."

"Ah," Moonlight said. "Their revolving pistols. With each partisan carrying at least two, they can get off twelve shots in the time it takes one of our regulars to fire his rifle and reload."

"Precisely," Blunt said. "The solution, I believe, is to have a squad of our own—your squad, Moonlight—armed with a weapon that is superior even to a brace of revolving pistols. Open the crate on the ground behind you, Captain."

Moonlight knelt and removed the lid to a wooden box that resembled a coffin more than a shipping crate. From it he removed a lever-action rifle with a brass receiver, one of a dozen tucked inside.

"Henry's Volcanic repeating rifle," Blunt said.

"I've read of them." The Henry was based on the Volcanic repeating rifle, but featured an improved action and better cartridges.

"The tubular magazine beneath the barrel holds fifteen brass-cased rimfire cartridges, and you can shoot them all as fast as you can work the action," Blunt said. "Forty-four caliber, with a practical range of four hundred yards."

"Surely not," Moonlight said. He shouldered the weapon, sighting down the long octagonal barrel at an imaginary point on the tent wall. He felt the weapon as an extension of himself, of his will.

"You be the judge," Blunt said. "You may have

six of the rifles, and two hundred rounds for each of your men. The remaining six are for my bodyguards."

Moonlight lowered the rifle.

"These weapons come dearly," Blunt said. "More than forty dollars each. If one of your troopers falls, see that the rifle is recovered. And don't give one to that red Indian."

"Of course not."

"Look here, Moonlight." Blunt stood now, and came around the desk, approaching so close that Moonlight could count the pores on the general's nose. "You may take any means necessary to accomplish your objective. You may use your own discretion, and I expect to have no further discussion regarding this directive, which will remain implicit between you and me. You are to report in a month's time. Understood?"

"Understood, sir."

"Also," Blunt said, picking through the papers on his desk, "I want you to be particularly watchful for a deserter and his brother who were participants at Baxter Springs. Odd, but reports indicate they made off with my Rucker ambulance wagon."

Blunt handed a report to Moonlight.

"The deserter's name is Frank Fenn. He was an officer with Halleck's command at St. Louis before he turned coat and joined his secesh brothers on the border. One of the brothers was captured and hanged, but the other is still causing a good deal of trouble."

"Yes, sir."

"I hate deserters, Moonlight," Blunt said. "I want you to place this Frank Fenn and his surviving brother just a little lower on your list than the Prince of Darkness himself."

"Sir," Moonlight said.

Blunt saluted, and Moonlight came to attention and returned the gesture, waiting to be dismissed. But the general paused, then placed a hand on Moonlight's shoulder.

"And, Captain," he said, "bring back my goddamned sword."

4

The trio of big Canadians turned and set their wings. Trudy Barriclaw remained still, clasped the revolver to her stomach with both hands, and watched from the corners of her eyes as the geese swirled down to join the flock already on the ground.

Trudy had been walking the banks of the brushy little creek, hoping to scare up a rabbit, when she heard the flock feeding among the brittle stalks of a nearby cornfield. The geese were noisy as they fed on the neglected crop, squawking and clucking contentedly among themselves as they picked kernels from the ground. The indistinct chatter of the flock was eerily similar to human speech, like the sound of a raucous party heard on a still summer night. Trudy wondered what it was that the geese were saying to each other, whether they were arguing about the route south or whether they were simply gossiping about their neighbors.

For the last ten minutes Trudy had been stealing her way up to the edge of the field, keeping low, trying to get within pistol range. The three big Canadians were a bit of unhoped-for luck, because they touched the ground on the side of the flock near her, not forty yards away.

Trudy dared advance no closer, even though the light was nearly lost, because there was no more brush separating her from the field. She thumbed back the hammer while holding down the trigger so that it would not make its alarming metallic clicking sound as the cylinder rotated into place, then released the trigger to stay the hammer when it was fully back. Lying prone, she felt the cold ground pressed against her thin clothes, making her empty stomach quiver. She extended the Colt with both hands, rested the butt on the ground, then peered down her right arm, lining up the sight cut into the hammer with the pin at the end of the barrel. She chose the closest bird, held her breath, and took aim at its bulbous head.

She squeezed the trigger.

At the crack of the pistol the bird dropped to its side, one wing flapping. Simultaneously the entire flock began to rise, a hundred birds filling the sky at once, and Trudy cocked the pistol again. In her exhilaration she followed another bird as it took flight, but prudently did not fire. Then she put down the pistol and ran into the field.

She placed her foot on the neck of the wounded bird and, shielding her eyes from the beating wings, grasped its feet. She gave a hard pull and felt the bones in the goose's neck stretch and finally snap. The wings slowed and then went limp.

She inspected the bird and noted with satisfaction the bloodstain on the snowy head. She grasped the wingtips and stretched the bird in front of her, but her arms weren't long enough to extend the wings fully. There would be many pounds of good, dark meat.

Trudy retrieved the pistol from the ground, lowered the hammer over the spent chamber, and slipped the gun into the wide leather belt that cinched her frayed skirt. She slung the bird by its feet over her shoulder. She whistled an old French tune her mother had taught her as she made her way back to the ambulance in the darkness.

Before Patrick Fenn reached Drywood Creek, he could smell it. The odor was a choking mixture of animals, food cooking over open fires, and human waste. He stood his horse on a slope over-looking the gentle valley for some time, studying the tent city at its bottom with a growing sense of disbelief.

Since the beginning of the war Drywood Creek had been a sleepy staging area for Union wagon trains leaving nearby Fort Scott, but seemingly overnight it had been transformed into a bustling refugee camp. Patrick had never seen so many ragged and hopeless-looking families in one place before. Most of them were Indians driven out of the Nations by tribes like the Cherokee, who had cast their lot with the South; the whites here had fled the violence in southwestern Missouri. Nearly all of them had come on foot, carrying their belongings on their backs and their children on their hips or trailing a few steps behind. They were to an individual hungry and dirty, and many of them were sick. And if they weren't ill when they came, they were likely to become so once they arrived: the unsanitary conditions that accompanied such an unplanned congregation of humanity was an ideal breeding ground for diseases ranging from diarrhea to diphtheria.

Patrick paused, debating whether he should continue down into the camp. Then he nudged Raven forward, reckoning that the Yankees would be reluctant to spare any soldiers on a cold October night to patrol such a mob.

"Hey, mister," a disheveled white man called

from the flap of a tent as Patrick rode into the camp. "Trade you my woman for that horse. She's ugly as sin, but she can cook some, and she works hard without having to beat her much."

The grim-faced woman beside him didn't look up.

"Not here for any horse trading," Patrick said.

"Then how about a poke?" the man asked, his face breaking into a yellow grin. "She's got some meat on her, not all knees and elbows, if you know what I mean. Got any cash money?"

"Who's in charge here?" Patrick asked.

"Why, ain't nobody in charge," the man said, and laughed, "This here's a democracy. We're all exactly equal—we got nothin' and we're goin' nowhere. Exactly what kind of mischief are you lookin' for, mister? Gamblin'? Whiskey? Whatever it is, I can find it for you."

"I'm looking for a piece of timber big enough to carve an axle out of," Patrick said, resting his hands on the saddle horn. "I reckoned on finding something along the creek bank, but I saw that all the trees bigger than a twig have been cut down for firewood."

"Gets cold at night," the man said defensively.

"Pay no mind to Dirty John," said a dark bald-headed man squatting near the fire. "He'll stick a knife in you and rob your corpse, first chance he gets."

"I doubt he'd get the chance," Patrick said,

unbuttoning his coat. Dirty John saw the butt of the pistol, cursed at the interloper, and closed the tent flap.

The man at the fire laughed.

Patrick swung down from his horse.

"We don't want no trouble," the man said. "You'd best keep on riding. Fort Scott ain't but a stone's throw away, and you'll find your axle there. Plenty of smiths and wheelwrights."

"Best if I didn't."

The man looked questioningly at Patrick.

"I'm a blacksmith myself," the man said. "Had a shop at Chetopa on Spring River. Then Blunt burned it and the rest of the town to the ground. Said it was a secesh hotbed. Well, he made it hot enough, all right. Where'd they burn you out of?"

"Cass County," Patrick said.

"At least you got a horse," the man said. "They took all of mine. Said they was commandeering them for the army, that they didn't have to pay me since they was spoils of war. Said I was lucky they didn't shoot me on the spot."

"What'd you do?"

"Shod the wrong horses." The man paused, took a chunk of greasy tobacco from his pocket, and deftly sliced off a piece. He had large hands, and forearms that rippled with muscle. Leaving the tobacco on the knife blade, the man held it out.

Patrick took it and, managing not to wince, worked it into his cheek.

"And I was born wrong," the man continued as he cut himself some of the tobacco. "My mother was a black woman who took a Cherokee, so that makes me a 'breed. Hell, I don't even remember her, but the whites don't trust me because of all the hell Stand Waitie is raising in the Nations, and the Osages hate me because they're mortal enemies of the Cherokees. That's why I shave my head."

"Thought you was young to have lost your hair," Patrick said.

"That's the point," the man said, and spat tobacco juice into the fire. "Scalping's not an Injun custom, you know. It came from back east, during the old wars, when the French offered a bounty for the hair of their enemies, proof they was dead. It sort of caught on."

The man offered his hand.

"My name is Botkins," the blacksmith said.

"Jefferson Davis," Patrick said as they shook hands. "Or, it may as well be. You manage to scavenge any of your tools after that fire, Mr. Botkins?"

"Some," he said. "Not enough to fill up my old carpetbag, but enough to patch an axle. I know where the last oak tree in the entire creek bottom stands—it's dead, but I reckon we can find a limb sound enough to use. I noticed you already got an ax."

"I can't offer you much," Patrick said. "Food,

when we have it. A fight, when we must. You're welcome to come along for as far as you care to. Leave when you like."

Botkins nodded.

"I'll get my bag," he said.

"Don't you care where we're bound?"

"Doesn't matter," Botkins said. "As long as it ain't here."

Frank Fenn stared into the fire beneath the sizzling goose and cursed his own fool recklessness. He had allowed himself to become spooked for no good reason, and there had been hell to pay for it.

"Stop it, Frank," Jenny said.

Frank mumbled.

"It does no good to dwell on it," she said, placing a hand on his knee. "We're together, and that's what counts. Patrick will be back at first light, and we'll repair the wagon and be on our way again. Nothing lost but a little time."

As she finished the sentence, snow began to fall, sticking to her hair and sleeve and melting in the fire.

"The meat is almost done," Jenny said, ignoring the flakes. "It smells heavenly. Trudy did a wonderful job, didn't she, darling? We couldn't have asked for better in the grandest hotel in Boston."

Trudy lowered her head and smiled selfconsciously. In her lap, gathered in a fold of her skirt, was a pile of down that she had saved from cleaning the goose. She picked through the down, her quick fingers removing dirt and flecks of dried blood.

"I'd hate for her to be shooting at *me*," Caitlin said. Little Frank was on her lap, staring longingly at the goose, and Annabel was fussing in the crook of her arm. "Trudy, slice some skin and a little meat off for the children. I know they must be terribly hungry."

Trudy gathered the down and tied it up in a kerchief. Then she took the knife from her belt and started work on the bird. She laid the steaming slices on a tin plate from Frank's kit, then took a bit of the meat, blew on it, and began to chew it finely for Annabel.

"Let's get the children into the wagon," Caitlin said when the snowfall became more persistent. "After we eat, we'd best get ready for the night. I think it would be useful to shelter ourselves beneath the wagon, with the canvas draped over the sides. That way we can put some stones together and have a small fire on the ground."

"Isn't that risking burning the wagon down around us?" Jenny asked.

"No," Frank said, rubbing his eyes. "Whoever is on watch can mind the fire as well. If we don't stand watch, we're liable not to wake up in the morning."

5

Trudy fed a handful of sticks to the waning fire in the little hearth made of loose stones at one end of their makeshift snow cavern. The wind had picked up during the night, and a steady stream of cold air poured in from the cracks in the wagon bed above and from the canvas sides. Still, Trudy thought, at least it was dry and tolerably warm—a measure better than sleeping on the ground.

Trudy resumed her work on the pillow she was making for Annabel from a kerchief and the down she had plucked from the goose. She had borrowed a needle and a card of thread from the housewife in Frank's kit. As she sewed she occasionally glanced at the sleeping forms around her and reflected upon how different she must seem to them. Frank and Jenny were holding each other in their arms, with Little Frank between them, and their expressions were almost peaceful. Even in these coarse surroundings Jenny's features were as refined as those of highborn ladies Trudy had seen in picture books, and Frank looked like a tired knight at rest in an illustrated plate from a Walter Scott novel. The child was a happy cherub that blessed their bond. Caitlin's ruddy complexion was deepened by the cold, and her red hair spread around her like a burnished crown, an Irish Madonna. The orphan Annabel, daughter of hanged brother Zachary Fenn and his ill-fated true love, lay uneasily near Caitlin's face. The infant's breathing had become ragged, her lungs betraying a rattle that disturbed Trudy. Judging from the smell, the baby also needed changing, but their supply of cloth scraps was running low and it would have to wait.

Trudy wondered what would happen to her—to all of them—if Patrick didn't return. She loved him desperately, but did not know how to act with him in front of the others. Alone, the expression of her desire was direct and uncomplicated, but in the presence of others she found herself fumbling for words and forever making groping gestures of affection that were seldom completed. Her dark skin and hair were a psychological barrier that prevented even the simple act of touching his hand, and openly declaring her love was a chasm she dared not cross. She cursed herself for not telling him how much she cared when he had left, for allowing cowardice to stay her tongue and leave her emotions unresolved. Life seemed more and more like that silver thread minstrels told of in song. What if Patrick's thread were to break? She didn't think she could bear to go on without him, to summon up the stuff that survival now demanded.

The Fenns were so unlike anyone she had ever known. Her father, a French trapper, had drifted easily in and out of her mother's life, leaving her an Osage squaw with child along the banks of the Missouri. It was something her mother had passively accepted, something she could not change, like the passing of summer into fall. But the Fenns—they seemed to have an unshakable belief in themselves and their destiny, a conviction that no matter what happened, they could face it and, by the force of their will alone, ensure the survival of the family. Hell itself might open before them, but heaven must surely await. Caitlin seemed especially certain that Providence had something better in store for them, but that type of faith was beyond Trudy. She had seen too much of the underside of the world to believe that any benevolence guided the hand of fate. Besides, Jesus and Mary were the reserve of those born white, not a half-breed girl who still read animal entrails as the portents of things to come. The white god was a jealous and bloodthirsty father who often demanded the sacrifice of his children. He had already taken the youngest of the Fenn brothers—would he require Frank and Patrick as well?

The sound of a horse trudging through the snow caused Trudy to place her sewing and her thoughts aside. She parted the canvas and crawled outside. It had stopped snowing.

A man on horseback emerged from the corner of the wagon. She could not see his face in the darkness, but his form towered over her.

"Patrick?" she asked.

"If that's what you want to call me," the man said. Trudy felt a quiver of fear at the man's deep, gravelly voice.

"What do you want?"

"A little food, a bit of warmth," the man said. "Whatever you're willing to give me, darlin'."

"I'm not your darling," Trudy said. "I've got nothing to share with you. No food. Be on your way."

"Your man leave you alone?"

"Yes," Trudy said, reluctant to betray the others. "Now go."

"Why are you in such a hurry to be rid of me?" the man asked. He swung down from the horse, letting the reins drop to the snow. "I've ridden a long spell tonight, and I sure could enjoy some company."

"My kind of company you don't want."

"That so?" the man asked, and stepped close to her. He reeked of sweat, tobacco, and cheap whiskey. She could see his teeth glisten in the light from the glowing canvas. "Kind of peculiar, a little girl like you out here all alone. Strange-looking wagon. Looks like it might belong to the army. Didn't steal it, did you? What're you hiding behind that canvas?"

47

Trudy was silent.

"Quiet all of a sudden, ain't you?"

He reached out and grasped her by the arm and pulled her roughly to him.

"Let me go or I'll scream."

"You scream and I'll cut your fool throat," the man said. He laid the edge of a razor against her neck. "I mean it. You keep quiet and I'll let you go when we're done."

With one hand, the man began to grope beneath her coat.

"Don't worry, I ain't going to touch you," he said as she squirmed. "I've had enough stinking red meat to last me a lifetime, and I could tell from the first you was an Injun by the way you *smelled*. Hello, what have we here?"

The man took the Colt revolver from her belt. Trudy's face burned with shame, both from the insult and from having lost the weapon that Patrick had given to her.

"I'll just take this with me, seeing as how you can't be trusted with it." The man slipped the revolver into his pocket.

The man's partner appeared, leading the team.

"Got things squared away, Bob?"

"Yeah," the partner answered. "Let's get the hell out of here."

"Keep to yourself until we're long gone," the man said, removing the razor from her throat and slipping it into his pocket. "If you don't, I'll come back and skin you alive. I've always had a hankering for a tobacco pouch made out of squaw hide."

The man hit Trudy with the back of his hand. She fell to her knees, the taste of blood in her mouth. The man laughed and turned toward his horse.

Trudy lunged after him, caught the man around the ankles, and dropped him to the snow. She scrambled up to his back, withdrew the knife that had been hidden in her sash, and plunged the blade into the side of his neck.

The man screamed and rolled over, knocking her off in the process. He clutched a hand to his bleeding neck and shouted for his partner to kill her. His other hand was fumbling for the pistol in his coat pocket.

Using both hands, Trudy drove the knife into the hollow between the man's neck and sternum. The man's shouting died in his throat as he fell backward, both hands on the knife blade, blood gushing between his fingers.

"Jesus," the partner said.

He dropped the line to the team and drew his pistol.

Trudy dug frantically in the dying man's coat for the Colt. She found it, but the hammer snagged on a hole in the pocket and she knew she would never have it freed in time.

Just as the partner threw himself down on

Trudy, a pistol shot rang out behind her, spitting a fountain of red and orange sparks into the night. The bullet struck the man in the shoulder, spilling him from the saddle.

His horse bolted.

The partner stumbled and began to chase his mount, trying to scoop up the reins with his good arm, but the horse insisted on trotting a few steps beyond his reach.

Frank Fenn parted the canvas and, holding the smoking revolver in his right hand, ran to Trudy. He jerked her away from the man on the ground and put a bullet into his chest. Then he turned back toward the partner, who had abandoned his skittish horse and was now running away as fast as he could manage through the foot-deep snow.

"Kill him," Trudy said.

Frank shook his head.

"Shoot him," Trudy pleaded, struggling to pick out the English words in the torrent of French and Osage running through her mind. "No time to be good. He'll tell others."

"It's too dark," Frank said. "It would be a waste of powder. At first light, I'll take one of the horses and follow him. God knows his trail will be easy enough to follow."

"If there's no more snow," Trudy said, regaining her command of the language.

"Frank?" Jenny called from inside the canvas.

"Everything's all right," Frank said.

Caitlin looked outside, saw the dead man on the ground, and quickly closed the canvas. "They've shot a wolf snooping around camp," she told Jenny. "Don't worry, go back to sleep."

"Wolf, my foot," Jenny said. "Frank?"

"Stay inside," Frank called.

Jenny parted the canvas.

"Good Lord," she said.

"It was a two-legged wolf," Frank said. "He's quite dead. Now please, get back inside and let us take care of it. We'll talk about it in the morning."

Jenny drew the canvas.

"Are you hurt?" Frank asked Trudy.

"Nothing broken," she said.

They knelt beside the dead man. Frank winced as Trudy withdrew her knife from his throat and cleaned the blade in the snow, then untangled the pistol from the fabric of his coat pocket. She put the Colt back in her belt.

"Help me drag him away from here," Frank said. "The ground's too hard to dig a grave. For all I care, the wolves can have what's left of him."

"No, we have to hide him," Trudy said. "We'll have enough trouble without explaining a dead man."

"Well, how do we get rid of him?"

"There's an old well near the field where I shot the goose," Trudy said. "We can dump him down it and nobody will ever find him, but we have to do it before sunrise. I'll go, because I can find it in the dark. You stay here and throw clean snow over this blood."

"I'll put him across one of the horses for you," Frank said. He grasped the corpse beneath the arms.

"Wait," Trudy said. "We need his things."

Frank paused.

"His coat and his boots."

"Powder and shot," Frank continued. "Maybe even some money or food. The other one dropped his pistol in the snow, and we need that, too."

Frank sighed.

"I've never robbed a dead man before," he said.

"He would have done worse to you," Trudy said as she stripped off the boots. "He would have killed all of us, even the babies. Besides, we have two more horses now. Go and tie them up while I finish here."

6

Sitting in the middle of a patch of cleared ground next to the ambulance, Trudy diapered Annabel with a strip of cloth torn from a man's shirt. She smiled and made nonsense sounds as she completed the job, but the baby fussed and coughed and refused to smile.

Trudy placed the infant on her hip and turned

her attention to the fire and the pot of boiling water that hung from a stick over it. She took a cloth bag from the pocket of the man's heavy coat she now wore, used her teeth to loosen the knot, and poured a handful of ground coffee into the water. The long-missed aroma blossomed in the air.

"Patience, littlest," Trudy told the baby as it nuzzled hungrily against her bosom. "You'll have to wait until your aunt Jenny wakes up."

Long before she saw it, Trudy could hear the sound of a horse breaking the snow crust as it approached from the south. After placing a reassuring hand on the pistol in her pocket, she squatted near the fire and waited.

Patrick and Botkins were riding double on Raven, and behind the horse they dragged a six-foot piece of timber that was as big around as a man's leg.

Patrick slid tiredly to the ground.

"It is good to see you," Trudy ventured.

Patrick nodded. He eyed the profusion of tracks surrounding the wagon, the patch of cleared ground, the strange horse staked with the team, and Trudy's ill-fitting but substantial coat.

"Trouble?" he asked.

"Yes," Trudy said.

"Soldiers?"

"No. A pair of two-legged wolves."

"Where's Frank?"

"Hunting," she said. "One got away. Wounded."

"I'll take some of that coffee," Patrick said.

"It is barely made."

"I don't care, as long as it's hot," Patrick said.

Still carrying the baby on her hip, Trudy scooped a tin cup full of the thin coffee and handed it to Patrick. Then she looked questioningly at the dark man.

"Thank you, but I'll wait a spell," Botkins said. "I'd best start peeling the bark off that timber. It's a mite green, but it'll have to do. Seems you folks need to get back on the road in the worst way."

Botkins took a quick measure of the broken axle, then stood astride the timber and went to work with the ax.

"Who is he?" Trudy asked.

"A blacksmith." Patrick explained the meeting at Drywood Creek, and Botkins's description of his circumstances.

"Can we trust him?" Trudy asked.

"We can't afford not to trust him," Patrick said, sipping his coffee and watching pieces of bark fly expertly from Botkins's blade.

"You look so weary," Trudy said, and she placed a trembling hand against Patrick's cheek. "Your eyes are very red. Why don't you rest now?"

"No," Patrick said. "Botkins is right—we need to be rolling again soon, and he needs my help to repair the wagon. Tell me what happened last night."

"They tried to steal the team. The dead one is at the bottom of a well a mile or so from here. Frank wounded the other, but it was too dark to see how badly. He ran away on foot. Frank took one of the captured horses after him. Captured horses are good, no?"

"Good, yes," Patrick said, draining the last of the weak coffee. "The bastards got more than they reckoned. I am proud of you, and later I want to hear the particulars of the battle. Now I've got to get to work."

He handed her the cup. His hand was shaking.

"Patrick," she said. "What is wrong?"

"Nothing," he said. "I am just being foolish."

"What do you mean?"

"I was afraid," Patrick said.

"You are afraid of nothing," she said emphatically.

"The man who is afraid of nothing has nothing left to lose," Patrick said. "When I rode with Quantrill, it did not seem to matter whether I lived or died. Now things are different—we have been given a reprieve—and I am allowing myself to care too deeply."

"Why is that bad?"

"There is too much at risk. Caitlin and the baby, Jenny and Little Frank . . ." He paused. "And you. I was afraid of what I would find when I returned here, and fear is a sickness that makes clear thought and right action difficult.

When a man wants something too much, that is precisely when he is most at risk of losing it."

"And what is this thing that you want too much?" she asked. "Perhaps you already possess it, perhaps it is something which you may take for granted."

"There is no such thing," Patrick said.

"Maybe so," Trudy said. "Clutch the mountain too tightly and you are sure to grow tired and fall. But people are not mountains, they are not stones—they are able to catch you when you fall."

"But the stone doesn't tire," Patrick said. "We have a long way yet to go. To keep the others from falling, I must become the stone."

The sun was three hours old and beginning to put a crust of glaze upon the snow when Frank and his unfamiliar mount crested a hill overlooking the Military Road. The horse was limping and in danger of throwing a shoe, so Frank dismounted and led the animal through the timber to the bottom of the hill.

"What's your name?" he asked the horse. "I've got to call you something. Something historical? Bucephalus, perhaps? No, I think not. You don't look much like a Pegasus, either. My brother named his horse Raven, which I always thought was peculiar—how can you name one animal after another? It didn't make sense to me, but I suppose he had his reasons."

The trail ended beside the road.

"This is no good," Frank said. "Partner here was a terrible thief, but seems to have made up for it with more than his fair share of luck."

Although Patrick could have discerned more, the snow made the story clear enough even for Frank to read: the partner had been favoring his right leg, but the ball must have passed through the fleshy part of the calf or thigh since it hadn't seemed to slow him down much; he had managed to dress the wound in some fashion, because the distance between the spots of blood in the snow had grown to several yards; and the footsteps ended beside a tangle of prints from well-shod horses, which could only mean Union cavalry. The horses had circled and gone back down the road the way they had come, toward Fort Scott. They would return in a few hours, and in force.

"Damn," Frank said, mounting the horse. He jammed his heels into the horse's flanks, urging it back up the hill. "Come on, you split-footed bastard. We're going to find out how far you can go before going completely lame."

Using the pieces of the broken axle as a guide, Botkins made a few marks on the bare oak log with a pencil. Then he tossed the pencil back into the carpetbag, stood with his feet planted over the work, and hefted the ax once more. The blade swung in a flashing arc over his right shoulder and made a sharp ringing sound as it bit into the hard wood.

"How does he keep from chopping his toes off?" Jenny asked.

"Faith," Patrick said.

Even though the temperature was barely above freezing, sweat gleamed on Botkins's naked scalp and dripped from the end of his nose as he worked his way down the timber. When he paused to wipe his head with the sleeve of his coat, Patrick gathered up the oak chips to add to the fire.

"Put 'em all in," Botkins said. "Make as big as a fire as you can, then let it burn down. The coals need to be good and hot, like a forge."

"Want me to spell you?" Patrick asked.

"Nope," Botkins said, shouldering the ax once more. "There'll be plenty of work for both of us soon enough."

After Patrick had fed the fire, he sat down on the oilcloth with Trudy's Colt. He removed the barrel and ran a patch down it to remove the fouling, then reassembled the gun and charged the spent chamber with powder and ball. Then he lowered the hammer into the safety notch between the nipples.

"Keep it clean," he told her. "It'll hang fire if you don't."

She nodded and placed the revolver in the pocket of her coat.

"Let me see the others," he said.

Trudy brought him the guns the interlopers had left. Patrick picked up the smaller of the two revolvers and examined it.

"Damn," he said.

"What's wrong?" Caitlin asked. She laid her Bible aside and, taking up her crutches, made her way over to Patrick. She peered intently at the weapons.

"It's a Lefaucheux," Patrick said. "Takes a cartridge with an internal primer. Did you find any ammunition for this? It would be packed in a box."

Trudy shook her head.

"Well, it's good for what's left in the cylinder, anyway—three shots. After that, we might as well throw it away, because we can't reload it."

The other revolver was a .36-caliber Whitney, all steel with ivory grips.

"This is better," he said. "Takes the same caps and balls as our Navy Colts. A well-made and serviceable weapon."

Patrick placed the Whitney in his belt and offered the Lefaucheux, butt-first, to Jenny.

"I think Frank would want you to have this," Patrick said.

"No," Jenny said. "I hate guns. The thought of keeping one on my person frightens me. Besides, I'm so ignorant of firearms that I'm sure it would represent more of a danger to myself than to any Yankee I might encounter."

"I'll take it," Caitlin said.

With her right crutch tucked up under her arm, Caitlin pulled the Lefaucheux from Patrick's grip and tested its weight in her outstretched hand.

"Cait—"

"What's the matter?" she asked. "Don't think a cripple can handle a gun?"

"It's not that."

"Then hush up," Caitlin said. Still holding the gun in her right hand, she pondered for a moment how to manipulate the crutches. Her mind made up, she threw the left crutch into the fire.

"It's best if I learn how to get on with just one of these," she said. "I can't afford to have both of my hands tied up, now can I?"

Caitlin shifted the weapon to her now-free left hand. With the remaining crutch taking the place of her missing leg, she hobbled back to her seat. She sat down heavily and placed the revolver on top of the Bible.

"Perhaps you won't always need crutches," Patrick said.

"I'd grow a new one if I could," Caitlin said, rubbing the stump. "Lizards can."

"They grow tails," Patrick said. "Not legs."

"I know," Caitlin said, "but a tail is something I don't need."

"It might help your balance," Patrick suggested.

"I'm pleased that the thought amuses you," she said. "Strange, but sometimes when I wake up I swear the leg is still there. I can feel it, all the way down to my toes, and it hurts like the devil. If I lie still and don't open my eyes, I can almost convince myself it's true."

"What I meant was a wooden leg," Patrick said.

"A peg leg like a pirate?" Caitlin asked. "Now, that would be very ladylike. I could get a hook on the end of my arm as well. It would be ever so dramatic."

"Cait, you have always been stubborn and hardheaded," Patrick said, "but now your tongue has become as sharp as a knife. I don't mind saying that it doesn't become you."

"Well, *I* mind you saying," she said, her eyes flashing. "It's bad enough being an old maid, but according to Mr. Patrick Fenn, now I'm a bad-humored one."

"Rubbish," Patrick said.

"Rubbish, is it?" Caitlin asked, then turned to Jenny. "I'm glad I'm not a horse, because my brothers would have shot me by now."

"I just meant—" Patrick stammered.

"I know what you meant," Caitlin said.

Patrick stood, muttered something about helping Botkins with the axle, and walked away.

"You musn't talk this way," Jenny said. She crossed to Caitlin and stroked her unruly red hair. "You are only eighteen, and so very pretty, so stop this nonsense about being an old maid."

"I've never been courted," Caitlin said. "I've

never had a gentleman call upon me, or bring me flowers, or read a poem to me from one of those silly books you go on about. The men in my life are my brothers, and the children I care for belong to them. I will never have a child of my own, and when I die, I will be alone. That's what I'm afraid of most—dying by myself, and being lowered into the earth to pass the ages alone."

"Truly?" Jenny asked.

Caitlin's lips trembled, and her face was red with shame.

"When the women's barracks in Kansas City collapsed," she said, "that terrible beam was on top of me and—and I couldn't move, I couldn't see anything, and I couldn't breathe. At first, I didn't know if I was dead or alive. After a while I was sure I was dead."

"Don't be afraid," Jenny said.

"That's easy for you to say," Caitlin said. "You have Frank."

"It won't happen."

"How do you know?"

"Because I won't let it happen," Jenny said.

"Why not?" Caitlin asked. "Why should you worry about what happens to my poor dead body?"

"Because not a single member of this family is more important than any other," Jenny said, holding Caitlin's face in her hands. "And even though you don't trust me, I love you as a sister. If it eases your mind to know that I'll be with you when your time comes—though I'm sure it's many years off—then I promise it will be so. We will be buried together. Inseparable. There'll still be room for Frank on the other side of me, and room on the other side of you for your husband. The men can go straight to the dickens if they don't like it."

"Do you swear it?"

"I swear," Jenny said, pressing Caitlin against her. "Even if I have to climb in after you and hold your hand."

Thomas Moonlight did not bother to knock the snow from his boots as he entered the one-room stone house that sat on a hill overlooking the Military Road. Once the house had been a welcome landmark, a resting place for travelers on the lonely frontier, but the family that had built it was long since gone. Now the structure was a lonely sentinel with vacant windows and abandoned furniture. A mound of snow filled the northwestern corner, where a hole in the roof revealed the winter sky.

A long-haired young man sat in a rocker in front of the hearth, a bandaged leg stiffly out in front of him, a rough military blanket on his lap. He was gulping whiskey from a tin cup.

Moonlight leaned his Henry rifle against a stone wall.

He dragged a wooden chair to the hearth and sat

backward in it, regarding the wounded man. Then he removed his gloves and took the cup from his hand.

"There's plenty for everybody, Captain."

Moonlight threw the contents into the fire, causing it to flare brightly for an instant.

"I want your head clear," Moonlight said, dangling the cup from the index finger of his right hand. "What's your name?"

"Russell."

"Your full name."

"Robert James Russell."

"Where are you from?"

"No place in particular," Russell said, looking into the fire.

"Give me an idea," Moonlight said.

"Family's from Independence," he said. "Been out west, before the war, to the Kansas goldfields. Went bust, of course. Sort of lived up and down the border since then."

"What's your occupation, Mr. Russell, besides being an itinerant fortune hunter?"

"Lately, my partner and I have been working as bounty hunters for the provost marshals in Missouri. Confiscating property and such."

"It's work that you seem well suited for," Moonlight said. "What is this partner's name?"

"His name was Powell. They killed him, and they shot me in the goddamned leg. Ask the soldiers. I told them the whole story."

"Tell me about the ambulance."

"It was military, all right. It looked like it had been through a real beating, like it had been rolled over or something. Also, it had a busted front axle. It wasn't going anywhere soon."

"And you and your partner, Mr. Powell. You were performing your duty by inspecting this vehicle and its curious occupants, is that right?"

"Yes, sir. We didn't get a real good look at them, because as soon as we came up on them, the shooting started. They all opened up with their pistols. There must have been five or six of them shooting at once."

"Who, specifically, was shooting at you?"

"A man and an Indian squaw. Some others inside the wagon, but I couldn't tell how many."

"I assume you returned fire. Did you hit any of them?"

"Well, it was dark. I couldn't tell."

Moonlight idly tapped the cup against the arm of the chair.

"Do you recall hearing them call each other by name?"

"No."

"How far across the line were they?"

"Not far," Russell said. "Fifteen, maybe twenty miles from here. You could find them real easy."

"With your help," Moonlight said.

"Captain, I'm in no shape to ride," Russell said. "Look at this leg. It hurts like the devil, and

I've lost a powerful amount of blood already."

"They tell me the ball passed cleanly through your flesh and that you are in no danger since the bleeding has been staunched," Moonlight said. He withdrew a stack of bills from inside his jacket, counted out a trio of ten-dollar notes, and stuffed them into the tin cup.

"Perhaps this will ease your pain," he said, offering the cup.

Patrick raked the spindle from the coals with a stick. Botkins scooped up the glowing piece of cone-shaped metal with a pair of tongs, placed it carefully on the end of the new axle, and tapped it snug with the head of the ax. Smoke curled up as the metal branded the high spots to be removed.

Botkins hooked the blade of the ax over the spindle's rim and pulled it off, letting it fall hissing into the snow. As Patrick raked it back into the fire to heat for the other end of the axle, Botkins went to work on the branded areas with a double-handled drawknife.

Patrick was about to add the last piece of the old axle to the fire when he stopped himself. He placed the narrower, splintered end of the piece on the ground and let it rest against his leg. It came up almost to his thigh. He grunted with satisfaction and placed the piece aside.

"This is the easy work," Botkins said.

"How's that?"

"The axle is pie," Botkins explained. "It's the wheel that worries me. One of the felloes and a couple of the spokes are broken. After those are fixed, the tire will have to be heated to expand it over the wheel, and we'll have to work together to get it fitted proper."

Patrick glanced up at the sun. It was already approaching the midpoint of its diminished winter arc.

"If it rolls," Patrick said, "it will be proper enough."

Botkins looked at him with a knowing smile.

"You want to stop in five miles and do this over?"

Patrick did not answer. His head was cocked, listening to the sound of a horse approaching from the west. He climbed up on the bed of the wagon for a better look. A man in an ill-fitting coat and light blue military trousers led a limping horse.

"Trouble?" Botkins asked.

"Keep working," Patrick said, jumping down. "It's my brother."

7

It was sundown when Moonlight and his command, led by the bounty hunter Russell, arrived at the spot on the prairie where the ambulance had been. They approached cautiously, sending Bone Heart forward to scout the area on foot. As usual, Moonlight had planned on attacking during the dead of night. But when Bone Heart returned from reconnoitering the area, he shrugged.

"Gone," Bone Heart said.

They found the snow well trampled. There were the remains of two fires and signs of much activity. A profusion of tracks surrounded the area, some leading in, others leading out. Some were made by the shod hooves of horses, others by human feet. Only two sets of tracks were fresh, however, and these followed different courses.

The ambulance had veered to the east, while the pair of horses had continued south.

"A choice, gentlemen," Moonlight told the troopers as he crouched in the snow, cradling one of the Henry rifles in the crook of his arm. "Do we or do we not follow the ambulance? What are the Fenn brothers thinking?"

Moonlight scooped up a handful of snow and squeezed it into a hard ball in his right hand.

"Wouldn't they stay with the ambulance, sir?" the sergeant asked. "I mean, they would want to protect their women, wouldn't they?"

"But the best way to protect the women would be to lead us away from the ambulance, would it not?" Moonlight said. "Or, perhaps, that is what they want us to think."

Moonlight stood and tossed the snowball to the south.

"A guerrilla fights best on horseback, not from the bed of a wagon," Moonlight said. "I don't believe it's a ruse. Gentlemen, mount up. We go south."

8

Thawed by the afternoon sun and then frozen by the cold of night, the prairie had become glazed with an unbroken sheet of ice. The hooves of the horses shattered the glistening crust as the ambulance made its way deeper into Missouri, with Botkins using the sliver of the rising moon for a compass.

In time, the prairie leveled out and gave way to what might have been a road, and eventually the road led to what in happier times might have been a town. Blackened foundations lined either side of the road, leading up to the toppled walls of a stone building in the center.

Botkins gently tugged at the reins and brought the horses to a stop.

"Where are we?" Caitlin asked.

"Goddamned if I know," Botkins said.

Caitlin slapped the top of his bald head.

"I'll thank you to watch your tongue," she said.

"And I'll thank you to watch your hands,"

he protested. "The next time you do that, I just might slap you back."

"You wouldn't dare strike a woman."

Botkins looked at her, then shook his head.

"You're right," he said. "You'd probably beat the daylights out of me."

Frank and Patrick drew up next to the wagon. Patrick patted Raven's neck while Frank fought for control of Splitfoot.

"This Nevada?" Botkins asked.

"No," Patrick said. "They burned the town but kept the Union post. We're not far from there, but this ain't it."

"It's all so quiet," Botkins said. "It gives me the jitters."

"It's not that quiet," Caitlin said. "Listen."

With pock-ets lined with silver, a pis-tol in each hand . . .

Even at a distance, the voice seemed full and confident and had just a touch of Arkansas twang. The melody was that of an old Irish tune the Fenns knew, but the words were different.

When-e'er I spy a pretty-little-girl . . .

"Where's it coming from?" Caitlin asked.

. . . with joy I do sit down . . .

"There's only one building left standing in the whole town," Patrick said. "It has to be coming from there, unless ghosts are doing the singing."

. . . with joy I slide her down!

"Don't joke about that," Botkins said.

"Ghosts," Frank said, "would sing on-key. What kind of a natural-born fool would be singing his head off in the middle of nowhere like this?"

"It's an invitation for trouble," Botkins said.

"Well, as long as we have an invitation," Patrick said as he urged Raven forward, "let's find out."

"Patrick!" Caitlin barked.

The singing continued as Patrick approached the ruined stone building. Then, abruptly quitting the tale of the roving guerrilla, the voice called out:

"Far enough, stranger."

Patrick stopped.

Frank placed his hand on the butt of his gun.

"Be you friendly or be you foe?"

"That depends," Patrick said easily, his hands crossed over the pommel, "on just how friendly you might be. No need for blowin' each other's heads off, is there?"

"If I'd wanted to kill you, your brains would already be on the ground," the man called. "If you're on your way out of Missouri, you're a mite turned around."

"We know where we're headed."

"Like hell you do," the man said, jumping over a pile of stones. "This here is Monticello. Nobody comes here anymore. That's why I like it."

He was a tall man with a sharp nose, a neatly trimmed mustache, and a pointed beard. He was wearing a Confederate officer's long coat, a hand-embroidered guerrilla vest, and a string tie cinching the collar of a ruffled shirt. His slouch hat was adorned with partridge feathers and his cavalry boots were splattered with mud.

In his right hand he carried a revolver.

"What's your name?" he asked. "Oh, it don't have to be your real name—just pick one. I'll give you one if you'd like. After all, I've got to call you something."

"Fenn. I'm Patrick, and this here is my brother Frank."

"Oho!" the man called. "Lordy, I believe you're telling the truth. Do you know how many soldiers the Yankees have looking for you?"

"We have an idea," Patrick said.

The man slipped the revolver in his belt. He whipped off his hat and bowed so low that his long brown hair nearly touched the snow.

"Thomas Jefferson Sweeney, at your service. Any enemy of that bastard Blunt is a friend of mine." Then he stood and replaced his hat.

"Are you alone?" Patrick asked.

"Alone, but never lonely," Sweeney said.

Patrick motioned for the ambulance to move up. Botkins clucked and shook the reins.

"My word," Sweeney said as the ambulance rolled up. "Which one of you is married to this redheaded angel?"

"She's our sister," Frank said.

Sweeney stepped up on the hub of the front wheel and lightly took Caitlin's hand. The motion was so swift, and Caitlin was so surprised, that Sweeney's lips had grazed the back of her hand before it was snatched away. If he noticed that there was no right foot beneath the hem of her skirt, he did not show it.

"Pleased to meet you," he said. "Pardon me for asking, but do angels have mortal names?"

"C-Caitlin," she said.

"Thank you," he said. "Now I have a name for the vision."

Sweeney jumped down.

"You always act so peculiar?" Frank asked sourly.

"I meant no disrespect," Sweeney said. "I was just being chivalrous. Surely you've heard of it. Or has the war robbed you of even the smallest of pleasantries?"

"You'd best take care with your pleasantries," Frank said. "I already told you, she's our sister."

"Hush up, Frank," Caitlin said. "You're acting like I'm some poor dumb cow with the family brand on its hide and this man is the butcher. In the first place, I am a match for rogues like Mr. Sweeney, or whatever his name really is. In the second place, I'm cold and the children are hungry, so let's not waste any more time defending my unblemished honor."

"Children?" Sweeney asked.

"Yes," Frank said.

"Well, why didn't you say so? There's one room

of this old church that hasn't collapsed yet, and we can get a fire started right quick."

They hid the ambulance in the draw behind the church, where Sweeney had staked his bad-tempered white mule, and in a few minutes a pot of what-have-you stew was cooking over a fire in the little back room of the stone church. In addition to the sack of potatoes and carrots, Sweeney had salt, sugar, coffee, cornmeal, and even a little dried beef.

The brothers exchanged knowing glances when Jenny asked where Sweeney had found all of the food.

"Gifts," Sweeney said, and laughed.

"Oh?" Jenny asked.

"The Yankees, I've found, are mighty generous when you ask them at the point of a loaded revolver."

"Mr. Sweeney, you are a rascal," Jenny said.

"I reckon it's all right," Caitlin said as she jiggled Annabel against her shoulder. The baby was exhausted from coughing and lay limply against her aunt, her chest rattling. "Lord knows they've taken more than food from us."

Sweeney took a cloth bag from his pocket and shook some brownish-orange roots into the palm of his hand. Then he took a tin cup, scooped up some boiling water from the pot over the fire and sprinkled the roots into the cup. The pungent odor of sassafras filled the room.

"Poor thing," Caitlin said. "She's running a fever, too."

"This will help the baby's cough," Sweeney said as he stirred a spoonful of sugar into the cup. "Let it cool a bit, then dip a rag into it and let her suck on it."

"So you're a doctor as well?" Jenny asked.

"Everybody in Arkansas knows a little bit about fixin' people up," Sweeney said. "Don't they where you come from? Pardon me, Mrs. Fenn, but I can't quite place the way you talk."

"In Boston," Jenny said, "we are more concerned with saving souls, I think."

"Boston!" Sweeney said with admiration. "That's a grand place. When I was a boy, I always dreamed of running away to Boston and stowing away on a ship, visiting faraway ports and maybe some of those islands where it is warm all year long and the natives don't wear a stitch."

"You would have made a splendid pirate," Jenny said.

"Yes," Sweeney said, "I would have. But I reckon I'm just a kind of land pirate now, hoisting the stars and bars instead of the skull and crossbones."

"My family—my grandfather on my mother's side, that is—was the master of his own ship," Jenny said. "The sea has been in our blood for generations, and I can't tell you how much I miss it."

"What about the other side of the family?" Sweeney asked.

"Preachers," Jenny said.

"Sailors and sermons," Sweeney said. "What a dangerous combination. Your family abolitionists?"

"Well, yes," Jenny said uneasily. "But that does not mean—"

"I suppose your grandfather, or his father, never brought a single slave across the Atlantic?"

"It was a long time ago," Jenny said.

"Of course," Sweeney said.

"Times change."

"I don't hold to the peculiar institution myself," he said. "Our family never owned any slaves, and we knew damned few families that did. It seems clear enough to me that slavery is morally wrong."

"Then why do you wear the Confederate gray?" Caitlin asked.

Sweeney laughed.

"Because the coat fits me," he said.

"Then you hold no commission?" said Caitlin.

"I have a field commission from Colonel Quantrill himself," Sweeney said. "I fight for Arkansas to be free from federal domination. In a few years, I believe, the South will free its slaves of its own accord."

"Many of them will have died in their chains by then."

"Perhaps," Sweeney said. "But many more will

die of starvation if they are simply let free, because they have no way of making a living. I believe in Jeffersonian democracy, madam; the human animal is never truly free until it possesses the means to make its own way in the world."

"Then you believe the slaves are animals?"

"We are all animals, every one," Sweeney said. "The strong dominate the poor. And if you aren't strong, you had better be special quick and damned smart."

Patrick took up the piece of broken axle he had carried in from the wagon and turned it over in the light, studying the grain. Occasionally he glanced at the contour of Caitlin's leg and the bit of exposed ankle beneath her skirt.

"What are you doing with that piece of trash?" Caitlin asked suspiciously.

"Just passing some time," Patrick said as he drew his knife. He tested the blade on the wood and found that the old oak was like iron.

"Here," Botkins said, handing him the carpetbag. "There's some better blades in there, and you can tap them with the mallet to get a bite."

"Don't get any ideas, Patrick Fenn," Caitlin said.

"Wouldn't dream of it," he said.

"You ought to take a measurement before you start," Botkins said.

"And risk getting clobbered?" Patrick asked.

"I'm not going to hop around on a peg leg," Caitlin said.

"You wouldn't hop," Sweeney said. He knelt at her feet and touched her skirt. "May I?"

"No," she said. "It's indecent."

"Not at all," he said, raising the fabric to her knee. "You should let your brother help you. Imagine having two feet beneath you once again. No crutches, no canes."

"But how will I walk?"

"A hinge," Botkins said, tipping his outstretched hand up and down at the wrist. "Where the foot meets the ankle. It might take some practice learning to walk with it, but as Mr. Sweeney says, no more crutches."

"No more crutches," Trudy repeated. She was sitting on the floor next to Patrick, her hands busily shaping corn dodgers for the fire.

"Just look at the line of this calf," Sweeney said, moving his finger along the underside of the muscle. "It is grace itself."

Caitlin blushed. She felt a strange sensation in the pit of her stomach, a tightening, and suddenly she was short of breath.

"You shouldn't touch me down there," she said, smoothing down the skirt with her free hand while cradling the baby with the other. "Besides, you don't really mean it. You just feel sorry for me."

"Oh no," Sweeney said. "Grandmothers and widows I feel sorry for. Never handsome girls with cheeks the color of strawberries and cream."

"Do you really think so?" she asked hopefully.

"Angel," Sweeney said, "I would be willing to lose some skin and hair over a girl like you."

"Stick around," Frank said. "You may get the chance."

Bone Heart was in the lead, with his aging double-barreled shotgun across the saddle. Moonlight was off to one side, a lantern in his hand. It was difficult business following the tracks at night over the frozen prairie. They moved slowly, pausing often to dismount and study the ground.

"There's something not quite right here," Moonlight said.

Bone Heart nodded.

"The horses never seem to get very far apart," Moonlight said. "Perhaps one brother is wounded, and is leading the other's horse. But I have seen no blood upon the ground."

Moonlight took a compass from his pocket and, holding the lantern high, took a bearing.

"They also are slowly turning, toward the northwest. Where could they be headed?"

"Nowhere," Bone Heart said. "They are making a circle."

Patrick was sitting on a large flat stone, his back against what remained of one of the church walls, fast asleep. His hands were clasped around his legs and his forehead rested on his knees, and he was softly snoring. When Trudy touched him he jerked awake and knocked her hand from his shoulder.

"It's me," she said. "I've come to keep you company."

Patrick rubbed his eyes.

"I was asleep," he said.

"I noticed," she said. "Why don't you go back to sleep? I'll stand watch for a spell."

"I shouldn't have been sleeping," he said. "In the army, they shoot you for that."

"In the army, they give you time to sleep once in a while," Trudy said. "Do you mind if I sit with you for a spell?"

"I'm all right," he said. "Get some rest."

"I'd rather stay and talk," she said, gathering her skirt and sitting with her legs beneath her. "I've missed spending time alone with you. Do you remember the things we used to talk about?"

"Talking is not what we did most," Patrick said.

"I miss that too," she said, leaning her head against his shoulder.

"Do you still read the cards?"

"No," she said. "I haven't done the tarot since that last time with you, just before you went away. It scared me too much. I decided that it wasn't best for us to know the future. . . . If you know something bad is going to happen, thinking about it and waiting for it to happen is worse than actually living through it."

Patrick put his arm around her.

"I saw you sometimes in my dreams," she said. "It was always at night, and you were always surrounded by flames. Men were dying."

"Don't talk about it," he said.

"No," she said. "It's over with."

Patrick was silent.

"It is over, isn't it?"

"It's over," he said. "I'm done with the war. The South is lost. I knew it when I heard that Vicksburg fell. But there's life waiting for us in Texas, away from all of this killing and dying."

"I want a family," Trudy said.

"You have one," Patrick said.

"I mean a family of our own," she said. "I want to start one right now."

She kissed him.

Patrick had forgotten how warm and wet her lips were, and how her body responded to his touch. He slipped his hands beneath her coat, fought clumsily with the buttons of her blouse, and freed her breasts. The nipples were hard beneath his thumbs, and her breathing became quick and shallow.

"I want you," she said. "I love you, I have always loved you, but right now I want you to—"

She used a common Anglo-Saxon word that Patrick had never heard a woman utter before, a visceral-sounding one that seemed to transcend language in its description of the sexual act. It was also the wickedest, and also the most powerful, word that Patrick knew.

"Are you shocked?" she teased.

"No," he said.

She took off her coat, one careful sleeve at a time, then let her blouse fall to the ground. She slowly unbuckled her belt and handed her knife and gun to Patrick. She stepped out of her skirt and removed her undergarments. Then she tugged off her shoes and her stockings.

Trudy walked slowly away from Patrick, balancing atop the stones. He watched the night shadows ripple over her calves and her buttocks, her dark hair swing across her back. Then she reached the end of the line of stones and turned gracefully on one foot to face him.

She crossed her arms behind her head.

"Do you remember," she asked, "how we used to be?"

Patrick gasped for air as his throat tightened and his chest swelled with emotion. It had been so long since he had allowed himself to feel anything that the sensation shocked him; it was as if he had been plunged into a cold stream on a warm summer's day. He felt as if he were drowning, sinking deep into the depths of his own soul, and the only person that could pull him back up was Trudy.

Later, wrapped in a blanket and lying warmly in

each other's arms, Trudy placed a hand against Patrick's bare chest. He roused.

"Promise me something," she said.

"Anything," he said sleepily.

"Marry me," she said. "Tomorrow."

9

It *is* a church," Patrick said.

"But we don't have a preacher," Frank protested. "It won't be legal unless we have a preacher, and that's not something we are likely to find anytime soon."

Patrick sipped at the cup of steaming coffee that Frank had brought. He looked to the east, where the horizon was smudged with the red glow of dawn. It should be warmer today, he thought, perhaps warm enough to begin melting the snow.

"Can't you hold off until we get to Texas?" Frank asked.

"Well, that's the thing," Patrick said. "She's afraid that both of us won't make it to Texas."

"What does she mean?"

"I don't know, exactly," Patrick said. "She's had some kind of dream, but she won't talk about it. Says she really doesn't understand the dream herself, just knows that it's some kind of omen."

Frank sighed.

"What could it hurt?" Patrick asked.

"It's not legal," Frank said.

"I don't care," Patrick said.

"It's not right," Frank said.

"Then what the hell is?" Patrick asked. "Do you think a piece of paper makes it right in the eyes of God? When there weren't any preachers, who do you think married Adam and Eve?"

"And they were thrown out of the garden," Frank said. "All of our trouble started with them."

"Yeah?" Patrick asked. "And we wouldn't be around if they hadn't gotten themselves kicked out by inventing all that knowin' and begettin' in the first place. I swear, Frank, you're acting more like an old maid every day."

"And you act just as foolish as you ever did."

"Sea captains can marry people," Patrick said. "Why can't army captains?"

"I'm not an officer anymore."

"Sweeney is. What about him?"

"Sweeney doesn't have a regular commission. Even if he did, I'm not sure he could do it. It's not like being the captain of a ship, where you're the ultimate authority for months at a time. You still need a preacher."

"What about civil servants?" Patrick asked. "Can't mayors do it? Judges and justices of the peace?"

"Well, yes."

"This is still a town, ain't it?"

"I suppose."

"Then what if we held an election and picked a mayor or a judge?" Patrick asked. "You know the law better than anybody. Wouldn't it be legal then?"

Frank put a hand over his eyes.

"You're turning me old before my time, Patrick."

"Think about it, damn you," Patrick said. "Surely there's got to be a way."

The first shot took the trooper to the left of Bone Heart in the upper jaw. The trooper managed to stay upright a moment, blood pouring down the front of his blouse, before he toppled from his mount. Bone Heart leaned far over and snatched the Henry rifle from the soldier's grasp as he fell.

Before the wounded trooper hit the ground, Moonlight and the others were returning fire with the repeating rifles. They were in a cut between two gentle slopes, and the fusillade was coming from the crest of the hill to their left. Black powder smoke billowed from a clump of brush as the attackers fired furiously at the Union cavalry, and the combined sound of gunfire echoed like thunder in the little valley.

One of the troopers landed on the ground as his horse was shot from beneath him. Russell had wheeled his mount to run when a rifle ball struck him between the shoulder blades and exited through his chest. He looked down at the bloody mess between the lapels of his coat, then fell into the snow, dead.

Then the ambush faltered, either from the attackers' need to reload or from their surprise at the rate of fire from the repeating rifles.

Moonlight gave a hoarse cry.

He turned Cerberus and spurred him up the hill while firing one-handed into the undergrowth beneath the trees.

Bone Heart and the rest of the squad followed.

Their horses broke through the brush and into a knot of a half-dozen terrified men in ragged clothes. Moonlight levered a fresh round and pressed the barrel of the rifle into the chest of the closest opponent, whose hands were still working frantically with shot and powder to reload his pistol. Moonlight pulled the trigger and the man was driven to the ground, smoke rising from his powder-burned jacket.

Bone Heart brought the Henry to his shoulder and shot one man in the back as he ran away, then turned to another man who was kneeling on the ground, his ramrod still in the muzzle of his Enfield rifle. As Bone Heart fumbled a moment with the unfamiliar lever mechanism of the Henry, the man seated a cap and brought the gun up.

They fired at the same instant.

The bullet struck the man at the base of the throat.

The ramrod pierced Bone Heart's upper arm.

Bone Heart's ears rang from the muzzle blast. He flexed his arm, teeth clenched against the pain, making sure that it still worked. Then he looked at the corpse of his opponent sprawled on the ground, his coat open and his shirt twisted up to reveal his painfully thin midsection, his head nearly severed from his body.

Bone Heart grunted, then spat.

Moonlight drew alongside. Spittle glistened on the dead man's hollow stomach. The other five ambushers were dead as well, arms and legs twisted at unnatural angles, a grotesque tableau of death upon the bloody snow.

"'God and your arms be praised, victorious friends!'" Moonlight shouted, holding the Henry rifle aloft. Then, somewhat softer: "'The day is ours. The bloody dog is dead.'"

Moonlight dismounted and studied the ramrod sticking through Bone Heart's upper arm.

"You are lucky," Moonlight said, grasping the end of the ramrod. "Nothing's broken." Then, in one long motion, he pulled the ramrod free of the flesh and threw it upon the ground.

Bone Heart's eyes turned upward in his skull and he slid from the saddle, unconscious. Moonlight caught him and lowered him down.

"We'll need a fire to cauterize this wound," he told the lieutenant, a young man named Hendricks. "I trust you still have that bottle of whiskey in your saddle wallets. I'll need it."

Then, to the others, he called: "Form a burial party for our dead. We can't afford to waste time by going back to post to deliver their corpses."

"Pardon, sir?" Hendricks asked.

"You heard me."

"But haven't we completed our objective?"

"None of these men match the description of the Fenns."

"But McAlester and Russell, sir," Hendricks said. "We can't just bury them here. What about their families?"

"Mark the spot," Moonlight said. "The army can retrieve them later."

"And the guerrillas, sir?" Hendricks asked.

"Gather their papers for General Blunt," Moonlight said. "The wolves can have the rest."

"I've studied it," Frank said. "I'm sorry, Patrick, but there is no way it would be legal."

Patrick was leaning against the stone wall, his hands crossed over Caitlin's Bible, his feet apart. Frank's hands were in his pockets, and he was looking away as he talked to his brother. Caitlin stood next to Frank, her left arm looped through his right for support.

"I'm no longer concerned about what is and ain't legal," Patrick said. "Legal means law, and laws change so as to make it convenient for the rich and powerful. Damn the law. I've spent my whole life being boxed in by laws."

"There are higher laws," Caitlin said. "There is God's law."

"That's why I asked to borrow the book," Patrick said, a little self-consciously. "I know I have never been religious like you have, Cait, but I can read."

Patrick handed the Bible back to Caitlin.

"Ecclesiastes," Patrick said. "Chapter nine, verse seven."

Caitlin found the passage and read for a moment. Her hands were shaking when she closed the book.

"That means what it says, don't it?" Patrick asked.

"Of course," Caitlin said. "But that doesn't mean—"

"That we can take it for true?" Patrick asked.

"But the law," Caitlin said. "You just can't say you're married and that will make it so."

"We can have a ceremony, can't we? That's the important part, isn't it, the public part? We don't have rings, but we can exchange vows."

"You need a preacher."

"I've had my fill of preachers, too," Patrick said. "They're as bad as the infernal lawyers, always twisting things around and deciphering them for their own good. Tell me how God's intentions can be clear to them and not to me, when it's all there in black and white."

"I don't know," Caitlin said. "It just is."

"Then maybe I ought to found my own church," Patrick said. "I can ordain myself as a minister, start thumping that book like I wrote it myself. Tell people that all the other religions are just so much swamp gas, and that I'm the only one who understands when the Almighty talks. That's the way it works, ain't it?"

"Pat, you're being a child about this," Frank said.

"Don't call me Pat. The only time you call me Pat is to remind me that you're the older brother."

"Dammit," Frank said. "You can't be arrogant enough to set yourself above the law and ordained religion, too. You're turning into a regular anarchist."

"You can call me all the low-sounding names you want," Patrick said, "but I know this is the right thing to do. I don't want to take the chance that I'll go under before we make it through the Nations. I want to set myself right."

"If you're afraid of God's wrath, then that's good, because we all should be," Caitlin said. "But there is time to make amends, time to do things right. This marriage of yours would just be a slap in the face of God."

Patrick laughed. "I'm not worried about roasting in hellfire," he said. "I reckon there isn't anything I can do now to make amends for the killing I've done. If I'm going to fry when my time comes, then so be it."

"There's time to change," Caitlin said.

"Maybe," Patrick said. "After we cross the Red River."

"Trust in God," Caitlin said. "Bide your time, hope for the best. Hold off on being familiar with Trudy until we can make it legal."

"Now, that would make me a hypocrite, wouldn't it?" Patrick asked. "You can stand with me, or you can stand against me. But before we go one step further, I am set on doing this one true thing."

"Then there's nothing left to talk about," Frank said. "We need to move, and we need to move quick. We've wasted enough time here already with that crazy bastard Sweeney. We're leaving in half an hour. You and Trudy be ready."

"Then I reckon you leave without us," Patrick said.

10

Patrick looked up and down the creek bank, then shrugged off his coat and spread it on the ground. He pulled his pistols from his belt and laid them on the coat, then quickly began to strip, beginning with his boots.

When every last stitch of clothes was piled on the ground, he picked up a bar of lye soap and made his way down the bank. The creek was frozen, but the ice was thin in the middle. He stepped out onto the ice, which groaned and spiderwebbed from his weight, and the soles of his feet burned. He felt particularly foolish, standing nude in the middle of winter on a sheet of thin ice.

He took another step and the ice broke. Patrick gasped. The water was waist-deep and bone-chillingly cold. Bending his knees, he eased himself down with his head and chest above water, then took a deep breath and submerged.

He surfaced in a spray of water, shaking water from his long brown hair like some kind of shaggy dog. He heard laughter from the bank, and when he rubbed the water from his eyes, he saw Sweeney standing there, holding a bundle beneath his arm.

"If you think it's so funny," Patrick said, "why don't you try it?"

"Oh, I've had my bath for the month," Sweeney said. "And it was hot. A tender young thing even scrubbed my back."

"I'll bet she did," Patrick said, applying the soap.

"I've brought you some things," Sweeney said, placing the bundle on the ground. "You and I seem to be the same size, and I have more clothes than I can carry. Hope you don't mind, but the trousers are gray, with yellow cal'vry stripes. The boots are damn near new; the Yankee who wore them had not worn them long before he lost 'em."

"Why are you doing this?" Patrick said, scrubbing his hair.

"Because I'm an idealist," Sweeney said. "And because I like you and that little Indian girl, despite what your brother says."

"Frank doesn't trust you."

"Nope," Sweeney said.

"He thinks you are scheming to dishonor Caitlin."

"Caitlin's a fine, strong-willed young woman," Sweeney said. "Your brother Frank ought to quit worrying and let things be. What Caitlin needs more than anything is a little attention, and I aim to give it to her. That raise any hackles with you?"

"You intend to stick around?"

"For a spell," Sweeney said. "Hell, you know what kind of lives we lead. You can't stay anyplace too long, or you'll find your neck in a Yankee rope."

"Come to Texas, then."

"I'll tag along for a while," Sweeney said. "If nothing else, it will annoy the living hell out of Frank."

Patrick boosted himself back up onto the ice. His teeth were chattering and his lips were blue. Sweeney threw a blanket around him and patted him on the shoulder.

"D-don't hurt her," Patrick said. "You do, and I'll bust you up twice as bad."

"I've never raised my hand to a woman," Sweeney said. "It ain't my style. I'll leave that to the marryin' kind, and stick to the business of keeping women happy. No offense, partner."

At midmorning they found the horses tangled in the scrub, exhausted, their bridles joined with a six-foot harness strap.

"Damn it all," Moonlight said. "I didn't think they would sacrifice two perfectly good horses on something that might not work."

"That's why it did work," Bone Heart said. His arm was in a sling, but the Henry remained across his saddle. "They are far away now."

"Yes, but we know where we left them and where they must be headed," Moonlight said. "Hendricks, bring me the map."

"Sir," the lieutenant said.

"Where do you calculate we are?" Moonlight asked, unrolling the map.

"Somewhere east of the Osage Mission," Hendricks said, indicating the spot on the map. "The Neosho River should be just over that series of hills, to the northwest."

"No," Bone Heart said.

"Then show me where we are," Moonlight asked.

Bone Heart ignored the map.

Instead, the Indian pointed with the barrel of the Henry to the southwest. "River is there, five miles maybe. Black robes are over here, two hours' ride."

"Good," Moonlight said, then turned back to the map. "Now, we lost contact with the ambulance here. They were heading east, but I think we can assume now that they will turn back toward the south and make all possible speed to the Indian Nations."

"They will already be there by now," Hendricks said.

"Perhaps not," Moonlight said. "They are traveling with a family, remember. I think it would be possible to intercept them somewhere here, along Spring River. It's a big stretch of water, and they are going to have to find a ferry or a place to ford it. With the snow beginning to melt, and the water rising, they won't chance losing the wagon. That means they will ferry it, which brings the choices down to two or three locations. If it were you, Hendricks, which spot would you choose?"

"Above Baxter Springs," Hendricks said.

"Correct," Moonlight said. "Sergeant, prepare the men to move out, double-quick."

"What about the horses?" Hendricks asked.

"The horses?"

"The pair," Hendricks said, indicating the animals still tangled in the brush.

"They would slow us down," Moonlight said. "But we don't want to leave them here for the enemy. Shoot them."

The brilliant winter sun washed over Trudy, decked out in white ribbons and a pale blue dress from Sweeney's trunk of wonders, like a spotlight as she stepped from the doorway of the church.

"My word," Jenny whispered. "She looks so different."

"Civilized?" Frank returned with a smile.

Leaning on Sweeney's arm, Trudy walked slowly down the path toward the others. She took her place beside Patrick, who looked equally foreign in his natty clothes.

"I'm not sure exactly how to start," Caitlin said, opening the Bible.

"Just get on with it," Frank said. "We're just doing this so we can get back on the road."

"Stop it," Jenny told him.

Caitlin opened the Bible to the marked page, cleared her throat.

"Well, we have come together to . . . *recognize* . . . the marriage of Patrick and Trudy," Caitlin said. "We humbly ask that this union be blessed by the Lord, and we throw ourselves upon His mercy."

Patrick took Trudy's hand.

Caitlin cleared her throat.

" 'Go, eat your bread in gladness and drink your wine in joy,' " Caitlin read, " 'for your action was long ago approved by God. . . . Enjoy happiness with a woman you love all the fleeting days of life that have been granted you under the sun. What-ever is in your power to do, do with all your might. For there is no doing, no learning, no wisdom in the grave where you are going.' "

Patrick kissed Trudy. She closed her eyes and savored the taste and feel of his lips against hers.

"I'm sorry I don't have a proper ring for you," he said. From his pocket he took a piece of leather whang string that he had braided into a perfect, intertwined circle.

He slipped it onto her right hand.

"Wrong hand," Sweeney said.

"Oh, sorry," Patrick said, quickly removing the leather ring and placing it on the fourth finger of her left hand.

"It's beautiful," Trudy said. "Thank you. I will never take it off."

"Now, I have something I'd like to read," Caitlin said, a little uncertainly, and began turning pages. "It is from First Corinthians, and it is something that I think that this family ought to try to remember."

Frank started to protest, but Jenny elbowed him in the side. Little Frank, who sat on the ground, clutched the hem of his mother's dress.

Botkins, who was holding Annabel, shifted uneasily.

Caitlin found the passage and smoothed the page.

"'If I speak in the tongues of men and of angels,'" Caitlin began haltingly, "'but have not love, I am a noisy gong and a clanging cymbal.'"

Sweeney nodded.

Caitlin continued, encouraged by his approval.

"'And if I have powers, and understand all mysteries and all knowledge,'" Caitlin continued, her voice becoming stronger, "'and if I have all faith, so as to remove mountains, but have not love, I am nothing. If I give away all I have, and if I deliver my body to be burned, but have not love, then I am nothing.

"'Love is patient and kind; love is not jealous or boastful; it is not arrogant or rude,'" Caitlin read. "'Love does not insist on its own way; it is not irritable or resentful, it does not rejoice at wrong, but rejoices in right. Love bears all things, believes all things, hopes all things, endures all things.'"

Caitlin closed the book.

Patrick scooped Trudy up in his arms, carried her to the back of the ambulance, and kissed her again.

Frank, who was already mounted on Splitfoot, led Raven over. Patrick took the reins and swung into the saddle. Sweeney was already on his white mule.

Botkins climbed into the wagon seat, then pulled Caitlin up next to him. They handed

Annabel to Trudy, in the back, while Jenny and Little Frank made their way over the tailgate.

Botkins took the reins in both hands and released the brake.

Frank gave ruined Monticello a last look, then whistled and touched his heels to Splitfoot.

Botkins flicked the reins and the ambulance rumbled forward.

11

They reached the ferry at Spring River, a few miles above Baxter Springs, late in the afternoon the next day. The sun had burned away all except the most stubborn patches of snow.

With Frank driving and Jenny sitting next to him, the ambulance wagon rolled down the graveled bank to the river's edge. The river was muddy and swollen. It was too wide to have frozen so early in the winter, but in cuts along the branches were pockets of ice and snow.

Sweeney and Patrick watched from behind the cover of the tree line high on the bank while the ferryman came out of his shack, pulling his suspenders up over his bony shoulders. A smokestack poking through the shake roof of the shack belched smoke, and Patrick rubbed his hands together, envying the disheveled old man for his comfort.

The man walked to within a few yards of the wagon, cut a plug of tobacco, and stuck it in his cheek.

"What the hell do you want?" he mumbled around the tobacco, then spat on the ground, wiping his chin whiskers with a greasy sleeve. "I was napping when the old woman kicked me out of the bunk and told me there were some fools in a wagon out here."

The broad-planked ferry rested against the bank in knee-deep water, tied securely with thick ropes to a cottonwood tree high up on the bank. The ropes were taut from the tension of the powerful current that otherwise would have been borne by the cordell. The cordell stretched from bank to bank, and its sagging middle was already skipping and slapping over the swiftly moving brown water.

"We need to cross," Frank said.

"Like hell you do," the man said. "River ain't been this high in a coon's age. We'd be likely to swamp before we get halfway across."

"You and your wife live alone here?" Frank asked.

"Find a clear stretch of bank and camp for a day or two until the river goes down some," the ferryman said, ignoring Frank's question. "I ain't about to risk my hide and my living on a fool's errand. Who are you people? That there is a military wagon, but you don't look like army to me. For all I know, you could be bushwhackers."

From the back of the wagon came a baby's hoarse cough, followed by a peculiar whooping sound as Annabel tried to force air back into her lungs through her mucus-choked throat.

"Sick kid, eh?" the ferryman asked.

"Yes," Jenny said. "She's my sister's child. We're bound for Fort Gibson and we need to get her to a doctor there just as soon as possible."

"Doctor won't be able to do nothin' for her that you can't," the ferryman said. "Give her some whiskey with some honey in it, keep her breathing. That's all you can do."

"You seem to know quite a bit about doctoring," Jenny said.

"I've done my share," the man said. "Have to, out here."

"Would you mind taking a look at the little one?" Jenny asked sweetly. "I'm sorry if my husband sounded rude, but we're at our wit's end. We just don't know what to do."

"No, thank you," the man said. "That disease is contagious. I've never had it, and I intend to keep it that way."

"We have money," Frank said.

"I don't know," the ferryman said. "It would take a respectable lot of money for me to take a look. I admit that I do make a poultice that is powerful good in treating whooping cough. Learned it from the Injuns."

"Please," Jenny said. "If you would only consider . . ."

"How much you got?" the ferryman asked.

"Five dollars," Frank said. "Gold."

"Ten might do it."

"All right, then," Frank said. "Ten."

"Let me see it first," the ferryman said. "I don't doctor on credit."

The ferryman stepped closer and watched anxiously as Frank's left hand went into the pocket of his coat. With his other hand, he pulled a pistol from his belt and placed it against the man's chest.

The ferryman raised his hands.

"Put your hands down," Frank said. "Act natural. I don't want that woman of yours to get ideas."

"Don't worry," the ferryman said disgustedly. "She ain't had an idea of her very own in twenty years. What you tryin' to do, rob me?"

"No," Frank said. "We just need to get across the river, is all."

"You might as well shoot me here," the ferryman said. "I'd rather die quick on dry ground than drown in that damned river."

"You're going to take us to the other side," Frank said, "and you're going to do it carefully. If any of the women so much as gets their skirts wet, I'll blow your brains all over that deck."

Frank raised his other hand and motioned for the others.

Sweeney and Patrick rode down.

"Get the ferry ready," Frank said.

"The old woman is going to think it's mighty peculiar," the ferryman said.

"Just do it," Frank said. "But remember, I'm watching you. If you misbehave, I'm going to shoot you. And if I miss, my brother here will finish the job."

"With pleasure," Patrick said.

"Bushwhackers," the man said disgustedly.

The lines were slipped and the ferry eased out a little, whipping the cordell taut. Botkins emerged from the wagon and, taking the team by the harness, pulled the hesitant horses up onto the ferry.

"Move it over, downstream," the ferryman told Botkins. "If we slip water, we'll all be gone under."

"Henry!"

A fat woman in a faded brown dress stood in the doorway of the shack, her hands on her hips.

"What now?" the man asked.

"Henry!" the woman called again. "Have you gone crazy?"

"Answer the woman, Henry," Frank said.

"Leave me alone, you flea-bitten hag," the man screamed.

"I told you to act natural," Frank said.

"I am," the ferryman said. "If I answered her polite, she would know for sure something is wrong."

The woman slammed the door.

Sweeney and Patrick dismounted and led their horses to the water's edge.

"They'll have to wait," the man said. "This ferry ain't big enough for all of you."

"It looks big enough," Frank said.

"You don't know sic'em about rivers, do you?" Henry asked. "If she were nice and calm, it might not be a problem. But look at that water shooting by. You have any idea of how much power it has? One mistake, and we're on our way to the Gulf of Mexico."

"He's right," Sweeney said. "We'll wait."

Frank nodded.

"All right. Let's go."

Patrick and Sweeney watched from the bank as the ferryman levered the winch and the craft began its journey. The river rushed loudly against the side of the ferry. The cordell creaked and groaned under their weight, and Frank was afraid it would part immediately, but it held.

The sound of the river drowned out the clatter of hooves high on the bank behind. Patrick shouted and swung up on Raven, but Frank could not hear him over the sound of the river. Patrick drew a revolver and fired into the air to get his attention. Frank cursed as he saw the troopers rush down the bank.

The troopers began to fire, and Sweeney's white mule went down, kicking and bawling.

"We're easy targets out here," Botkins said.

"Get down," Frank shouted to the wagon. "Lay flat."

The ferryman laughed.

Frank hit him squarely in the teeth with his fist, lifting him from the deck of the ferry. He landed in the water with a splash, his arms waving wildly.

Standing flat-footed, Sweeney drew both of his revolvers and began firing. One of the troopers toppled from his horse while the others fought their unsteady mounts down the steep bank, trying to bring their rifles to bear. Moonlight was screaming for them to dismount and take aim.

"Hold the team," Botkins shouted to Frank, then snatched the ax from the back of the wagon. The blacksmith planted his feet and took a wide swing at the cordell, pinning it against the lever mechanism used to winch the ferry across. The rope quivered like a bowstring and then parted with a snap.

The ferry shot down the river.

Botkins fell to his stomach as bullets from the Henry rifles bit chunks of wood from the deck. The team was spooked, and the wagon rocked forward and back, the locked rear wheels sliding on the deck.

"My God," Frank gasped. "They have repeating rifles."

"Hold the team," Botkins called as he crawled on his knees and elbows to where Frank crouched, struggling with the horses.

On the bank, Patrick spurred Raven forward. He stuck out his right hand as he approached Sweeney, who grabbed on and pulled himself up behind.

"The bastards killed my mule!" Sweeney shouted.

Raven raced down the river's edge, his shoes clattering on the river rock. As they raced past the shack Henry's fat wife stuck the muzzle of a double-barreled shotgun out the door and pulled both triggers.

"Patrick!"

Trudy had seen them both fall from Raven, and she was climbing over the tailgate of the wagon. Jenny seized her around the middle with both hands and hauled her back inside.

"Let me go," Trudy cried.

"You'll get yourself killed," Jenny said, pulling her down to the wagon bed.

The ferry slipped behind an island in the middle of the river.

Patrick got to his knees. The riverbank was lower here below the shack, and for a moment they were shielded from the bullets of the troopers.

"I ain't never killed a woman before," Patrick shouted, drawing his pistol, "but now seems like a good time to start."

The fat woman slammed the door of the shack.

Sweeney had rolled down the bank to the river, and he lay with one foot in the water. He pulled himself up and touched a hand to his bloody right cheek, which was peppered with tiny puncture wounds.

"Birdshot," he said.

Patrick whistled and Raven trotted over. As he put his foot in the stirrup Sweeney called to him.

"Go," Sweeney said. There was a skiff on the bank, and Sweeney had cut its rope. "They'll catch us both right quick riding double."

Sweeney pushed off hard from the bank and hopped into the bow of the little flat-bottomed boat. As the river carried it away Sweeney took the middle seat, unshipped the oars, and began to row.

Patrick used his quirt and Raven bolted.

The ferryman stumbled out of the river, his chest heaving, and looked longingly down the river as his ferry disappeared around the bend. It was soon followed by the skiff.

"You're under arrest," Moonlight said, scrambling down the bank on foot with his troopers.

"Like hell I am," the ferryman said, digging in his pocket for the tobacco. His wife brought a blanket from the shack and draped it over his shoulders.

"You've provided aid and comfort to the enemy."

"You fat-headed sonuvabitch," the old man said. "They shoved a gun in my face. Now they've taken off with damn near everything I own."

"He's got a point, sir," Hendricks said.

Moonlight cursed.

"Orders, sir?" the sergeant asked, his rifle in the crook of his arm. "Should we give chase?"

"You'll never catch 'em," the ferryman said. "The bank turns rocky a few miles downriver, and you would have to be able to fly like a bird to match their speed."

Moonlight whipped off his hat, threw it on the ground, and stomped on it.

Bone Heart laughed.

He had never seen Moonlight give vent to his emotions before—in fact, he had not been convinced that the bluecoat leader *had* emotions—and here he was, acting like a madman, flattening the crown of his chief's hat.

"Should we follow the rascal that got away, sir?" the sergeant asked.

"No," Moonlight answered. "We'll stay on the wagon. The river's taking them straight into the Nations. Since we don't know where they might jump off, we'll cross the river at the first opportunity and pick up the trail when we can."

"You got only one thing left going for you," the ferryman said.

"And what is that?" Moonlight asked.

"There's a good chance they'll drown."

The ferryman spat.

12

Sweeney put his back into the oars and gradually closed the distance between the skiff and the ferry. When he was close enough, he threw the bowline to Botkins, who hauled the skiff up close and tied it fast.

"Let us have those," Botkins called.

Sweeney tossed the oars over, then climbed from the skiff onto the deck of the ferry. They were close to the eastern bank, and the ferry was slowly rotating as it rode the current.

Botkins handed one of the oars to Frank.

"We're going to have to get straightened out," Botkins said. "If we come up against a towhead, we'll be swamped. Stand over on that corner, and I'll stand here. Just dip the oar in, try to use it as a rudder."

Frank dipped the oar into the water. The water throbbed against the blade. By coordinating his actions with Botkins, they managed to stop the rotation of the raft.

"Good," Botkins said. "Now let's get it back out

in the middle, away from the bank. Sweeney, there's a coil of rope there on the deck. Lash the wagon down the best you can."

Sweeney nodded and went to the rope.

"Where's Patrick?" Trudy asked.

"He's all right. We got hit with a double load of birdshot, but it was more of an insult than anything."

"Your face is bleeding."

"It itches," Sweeney said.

Trudy searched the bank, but saw no sign of Patrick. The terrain had begun to change. The gently rolling hills around Baxter Springs had been replaced by steep, rocky bluffs the color of rusted iron.

"He's a resourceful lad," Sweeney said. "He'll catch up with us later."

When Sweeney had finished tying down the wagon, he allowed Caitlin to clean his face with a cloth dipped in river water. The bleeding had slowed, but a half-dozen pieces of birdshot remained under the skin.

"What a ride," Sweeney said.

"Does this amuse you?"

"It beats farming, angel."

"Those pellets will have to come out," Caitlin said. "They'll make you sick. I'm sorry, but we don't have any whiskey. You'll just have to grit your teeth."

Caitlin took a needle from the sewing kit. She

asked Sweeney to lie down, and she eased herself down on the deck next to him, resting his head in her lap.

Sweeney looked up at her and grinned.

"If I'd known this was the treatment," he said, "I'd have got shot right from the start. Go right ahead, madam doctor, I am ready. If the operation isn't successful, I'll die a happy man."

Caitlin probed a little deeper with the needle than she had to. Sweeney flinched.

"Now, that hurt," he said.

"I meant it to," she said.

Caitlin worked carefully, nudging each of the lead pellets to the surface with the point of the needle.

"Is that all of it?" she asked, lifting the hair behind his ear and inspecting his neck.

"My clothes protected most of me," he said.

"Good thing only your poor wooden head was exposed," she said. "Wait. Here's another, just behind your ear."

When she was done, she gathered up the birdshot and showed it to Sweeney.

"Not enough to kill this partridge," Sweeney said, inspecting the contents of her palm. Holding her hand in both of his, he closed her fingers and kissed her wrist.

"You're lucky it wasn't buckshot."

Caitlin drew her hand away and threw the birdshot into the water. Sweeney's cheek was spotted with blood, and she wiped it away, then smoothed his hair with her palm.

"Do you really think Patrick will be all right?"

"Of course," Sweeney said. "It's us I worry about. Those Yankees had repeating rifles. We're safe for now, but it won't be long before they cross the river. If it comes down to a shooting match when they catch up with us, we're goners."

"Surely they won't follow us down into the Nations."

"Not normally," Sweeney said. "But these troops are different. Did you see how they stood their ground when Patrick and I returned fire? I don't think they're scared of any—"

"Hang tight!" Botkins called.

The ferry slammed against an uprooted tree that was snagged diagonally in the channel, its roots held fast by a jam beneath the surface. The deck of the ferry tilted downriver as the current surged against it. Water slipped over the side, soaking Caitlin and Sweeney, and lapped at the wheels of the wagon.

Caitlin began to slide across the deck.

Sweeney grabbed a wagon spoke with one hand, and as Caitlin tumbled toward the river he snatched her up with the other. "Hold on," he instructed her as he went to help the others.

"Push off!" Botkins called, and he and Frank worked frantically against the log with the oars. The ferry pivoted, but would not quite come free.

Frank's oar snapped, leaving him with a useless bit of handle.

Sweeney dropped over the side of the ferry and wedged himself between it and the snag. He brought up his feet, planted both of his boots on the trunk of the tree, and pushed.

Sweeney fell into the water as the ferry broke free of whatever branch had held it fast. As the craft resumed its headlong dash down the river, Sweeney bobbed in the water behind, coughing and trying to stay afloat against a current that seemed intent on pushing him under.

Botkins threw a coil of rope over the side.

Sweeney grabbed the rope as it snaked out behind the ferry, and Botkins hauled him in. He lay for a moment coughing and sputtering on the deck, then began to laugh.

"I can't swim," he said.

Patrick followed the river south into the Cherokee Nation.

The ground became increasing rocky, and when night came he stopped, not wanting to risk the chance of breaking one of Raven's legs in the darkness. There was no sign that he was being followed.

He staked Raven at the bottom of a high cliff, slung his bedroll over his shoulder, and began to climb. He found a shelf about thirty feet above the ground, and toward the back he found a small cave carved into the cliff. The cave could not be seen from the ground.

From the lip of the shelf he could survey the trail that ran alongside the river for a hundred yards in either direction, and he had a good view of the area where Raven was staked.

The floor of the little cavern was hard-packed clay, and it went deep into the hillside, so deep that Patrick could feel the warmth of the earth. There were animal tracks in the clay, mostly raccoon and possum, but no sign that the cave had been visited by a human being within memory of the clay.

Patrick made his bed and stripped to his long red underwear, not wanting to sleep in the fine clothes Sweeney had given him. The night was still and the sound of the river flowing nearby was soothing, but although he was exhausted, Patrick could not sleep.

He sat up, fumbled in his kit, and lit a candle. He stuck the candle upright into the hard clay, then lay back down with his hands behind his head.

The ceiling of the cave was covered with pictures.

The ferry came to rest against a gravel bar on the eastern bank, in an eddy of calm water that belied the fury of the rest of the river.

The sun had been down for an hour and the journey had become a frightening series of unseen snags and traps. They had nearly swamped twice more, but had managed to free themselves both times.

"We made it," Botkins said, almost in disbelief. He stuck the blade of the remaining oar into the sandbar.

"Can we get the wagon off?" Frank asked.

Botkins jumped off onto the bar.

"Yes," he said. "The bank isn't too steep here, and the ground seems to be solid enough."

When the team had pulled the wagon onto the bar, Botkins and Sweeney pushed the ferry back into the river. They waded out until the current took hold of it again, and it quickly disappeared into the darkness.

At first Patrick thought the pictures were the work of a child, because they lacked perspective and seemed all jumbled together. They were in colors one would expect to find close at hand: vermilion, charcoal, chalk. There were circles, spirals, and triangles. Stick figures hunted great stick beasts. And at one spot, high upon the wall where the rock was smooth, was the outline of a human hand.

Patrick took up the candle and inspected the outline. Someone long ago had very carefully traced his own hand upon the rock, starting alongside one wrist and going over each of the fingers and thumb until arriving again at the wrist.

He extended his own hand, fingers out-stretched, and placed it inside the outline. The rock was cold like the grave. He felt a strange chill, knowing that the individual who had made the outline was long since dead. He had heard talk of the civilizations that flourished in America before the coming of Columbus, even before the coming of the known Indian tribes. Was the unknown artist a member of one of the lost tribes of Israel? He doubted it. The symbols looked nothing like the Hebrew letters he had seen in books.

He removed his hand from the rock.

Patrick took a piece of flint from the floor of the cave and began a drawing of his own hand beneath the one on the wall. He made a wagon, with crossed circles for wheels. Behind the wagon he drew Caitlin and Jenny and Trudy—Caitlin had only one leg, and all wore triangles for dresses—and two diminutive figures, for Little Frank and Annabel. He placed himself and his brother in front of the wagon, stick men mounted on stick horses. Finally he added the Big Dipper in the sky above, and from the handle of the dipper he drew an arrow, indicating their passage south.

13

Trudy looked longingly behind her at the river as the team pulled the ambulance up the bank toward the dark wood. Her thumb was gently rubbing the braided leather ring on the fourth finger of her left hand.

"I should wait," she said.

"We can't leave you here by yourself," Jenny said.

"How will Patrick know where to find us?"

"He will find us. You must have faith."

"Faith," Trudy mused. "That's a word the preachers use when they want you to believe in something you can't see."

The wagon seemed to be swallowed by the woods as it followed the trace south. Branches scratched against the canvas sides and the wheels bumped over the rocky ground. There was no conversation among them as they went, and the only sounds other than those of the horses and the wagon were the terrible coughs of the infant.

Toward midnight it began to rain, gently at first, and then with more force. The wet air aggravated the baby's condition, and her coughing became a shrill bark.

Then she began to vomit.

Jenny held the baby upright on her shoulder,

patting her back, wiping the vomitus from her mouth and nose, and keeping up a steady patter of little nonsense words whispered into the sick child's ear.

Annabel was running a fever. Her head was like an oven against Jenny's shoulder, and her tiny eyes were rimmed in red. Her nose was crusted with mucus. The baby struggled, fought for breath, and quit breathing.

"Come on, little one," Jenny said. "I know you're tired, but please, don't give up."

Jenny placed Annabel on her lap and jiggled her. She worked her arms back and forth in a frantic game of pattycake, then blew gently on her face.

The baby refused to breathe. Her lips were turning blue.

Jenny was frightened. Caitlin was asleep, and Sweeney was riding up front with Botkins.

"Frank!" Jenny called. "I need help!"

The baby's face was a deepening purple.

"What do we do?" Trudy asked.

"I don't know," Jenny said.

Botkins brought the team to a halt. Sweeney crawled through the canvas into the back of the ambulance. He did not have to ask what was the matter. He knelt beside Jenny, took a flask of whiskey from inside his coat, and poured some into the palm of his hand.

"Open her mouth," he said.

Trudy opened the baby's mouth and Sweeney

held his cupped hand beneath her nose. Annabel started a bit, then Sweeney poured the whiskey into her mouth. It dribbled from his palm down her chin.

The whiskey burned her throat. Annabel jerked her head back, held her mouth wide in anger for a long moment, then took a great whooping breath.

"Jesus and Mary," Sweeney said.

He began to hoist the flask, but Jenny snatched it from him.

"Annabel needs it more than you," she said. "Besides, you should have told us earlier about it."

Frank parted the canvas.

"We've got to get the baby some help," Jenny said.

After another hour of traveling in the rain, they came upon a cabin. The cabin was in a small clearing, and over the clearing drifted a layer of wood smoke. Frank held up his hand and Botkins brought the wagon to a halt.

"Let's go around," Botkins said.

"You have ears," Frank said. "That baby is going to die if we don't find some help."

"But we don't know who is in that cabin," Botkins said.

"It doesn't matter," Frank said. "We have to do something."

"We're likely to get shot, knocking on some-body's door in the middle of the night."

"We're not going to knock on the door," Sweeney said, jumping down from the wagon. "And we're not going to give them a chance to shoot back."

"I'm not going to bust into somebody's home," Frank said. "We'll ask for help."

"Don't do it my way," Sweeney said, "and you're either going to be shot from your horse right off, or you're going to spend an hour standing in the rain arguing at a locked door."

"He's right," Caitlin said. "This baby needs to be warm and dry."

"If we're lucky, the rain has covered the sound of our approach," Sweeney said. "Frank, you stay right where you are and look sharp. I'll go introduce ourselves."

Sweeney took off his shoes and threw them up into the bed of the wagon, then padded along the path toward the front door. The cabin was dark, although smoke still curled lazily from the rock chimney.

Sweeney crept up on the porch and drew his revolver.

The door opened.

"Put away your gun," a voice called. "Why do you sneak up on me like a thief in the night, when everything I have is welcome to you?"

"Step out," Sweeney said.

An old man took two steps out onto the porch, his hands open at his sides.

"Do you want me to raise my hands?" he asked. "Would that make you feel better? Stop this foolishness and bring the child inside."

"How do you know about the baby?" Sweeney asked.

"How could one not know?" the man asked. "I've listened to her cough for most of the night. It began in a dream, I think, but I do not think I am dreaming now."

He turned and walked back into the cabin, leaving the door open and Sweeney standing with his revolver pointing at nothing. With great care, the old man lit a coal-oil lamp with a stick of kindling from the fireplace, then replaced the globe and turned up the wick.

The old man's face was revealed in the orange flame. His skin was like cracked and hardened leather that had been left out in the rain. His hair was white, but his dark eyes were clear.

"What kind of Indian are you?" Sweeney asked. His eyes darted around the interior of the cabin.

"My name is John Greenfeather," the old man said. "I am Cherokee, of course. Please stop looking, because there is nobody here but me. My two wives are out back, buried near the orchard, but I can almost promise you they will be no trouble. I have three sons, but they are all away. Two of them fight with Stand Waitie."

Jenny appeared at the doorway, cradling Annabel in her arms.

121

"Can you help us?" she asked. "She has stopped breathing once already, and I am afraid if she does it again, we will not be able to bring her around."

"Please, bring the child inside," Greenfeather said. "Tell the others to come as well. It is not a night to be sleeping out-of-doors."

"Thank you," Jenny said.

"I don't get much company these days," Greenfeather said. He went to a row of shelves that lined one wall of the cabin and began lifting tins and boxes, shaking them, opening their lids and probing their contents with his fingers. "I have a little coffee, some tobacco, but no whiskey."

"Do you need whiskey?" Jenny asked. "We have this."

She held out the flask and the old Indian took it, unscrewed the lid, and waved it beneath his nose.

"Good," he said.

He picked a tin cup from the shelf, shook the dust out of the cup, and poured it half full of whiskey.

"Can you make something to help her?" Jenny asked hopefully.

"Yes," Greenfeather said.

He drank the whiskey, all of it.

"Whoa," Sweeney said.

Greenfeather held up his hand, smacking his lips.

"That portion was for the doctor," Greenfeather

said. "It helps me think. Here is some coffee. The pot is over there by the stove. Fetch some water from the well and put it on to boil."

"Is that for the doctor as well?" Caitlin asked.

"It is for all of us," Greenfeather said. "It will be a long night."

Jenny handed the pot to Sweeney.

"Why do I have to go back out into the rain?" he asked.

"Because Frank and Botkins are busy with the horses," Caitlin said. "And because it would be the gentlemanly thing to do."

"Talk to me while I work," Greenfeather said.

"What are you looking for?" Jenny asked.

"A dried plant," Greenfeather said. "It is here somewhere, if only I can remember which tin. . . . Ah, here it is."

"What is it?"

"Horseheal," Greenfeather said, dipping his fingers into the powdery substance and bringing it to his nose.

"I thought that was only for patching up horses," Caitlin said.

"It is for many things," Greenfeather said. "The root is useful in treating coughs, fevers, and diseases of the lungs. It is not native to this region—but then, neither am I. My people brought it with them when they came from the faraway home."

"Will it cure her?" Trudy asked.

"The only cure for her cough is time," Greenfeather said. "But this will fight the fever and help bring air into her lungs by opening her throat."

Sweeney came back with the pot of water, and Greenfeather dipped a little into the cup. Then he poured a bit of the powder into it and mixed the watery paste with a spoon.

"I don't think we'll be able to get it down her," Jenny said.

"What is her name?" Greenfeather asked.

"Annabel."

"It is musical," Greenfeather said. "Is she your child?"

"No," Jenny said. "The little boy is mine. The baby is the child of my brother-in-law and his . . . wife. They are both dead. They were killed in the same accident that took her leg."

"Were they good people?"

"I don't know what good is anymore," Jenny said.

"They were good," Caitlin said. "Worse than some, perhaps, but a good deal better than many."

Greenfeather plucked a straw from a broom that stood in the corner. He cut it down to four inches, then held it lengthwise up to the lamp. Then he blew through it, and was satisfied at the rush of air.

"She is fortunate to have aunts such as yourself," Greenfeather said. He pronounced *aunt* as

Jenny did, with the soft eastern sound that sounded somewhat peculiar to western ears.

"Are you from the east?" Jenny asked.

"Aren't we all?" Greenfeather returned with a smile. "Always from the east, from the morning, moving into darkness. But that is not quite what you asked. Yes, I am from back east, from Georgia, where I was a great man before the feud. I owned a large house, and slaves, and my voice was respected. Can read and write—both Cherokee and English. I was part of my nation's delegation to the liars in Washington. Oh, if only we had had the wisdom of our wild brothers on the plains. Now? Just another old man waiting for the sun to set."

Greenfeather put the straw in his mouth and sucked it full of the watery paste from the tin cup.

"Hold the baby quite still, please."

"What are you going to do?" Jenny asked.

"Give her the medicine, of course," Greenfeather said.

Greenfeather again put the straw in his mouth and gently pinched the baby's nostrils together. The baby fussed, then after a moment she opened her mouth. He leaned quickly forward and inserted the straw to the back of her throat, puffed the medicine in, then held her mouth closed until she swallowed it.

"Now, if she doesn't throw it up, your little Annabel here should begin to feel better shortly.

We will give her some more just before dawn."

"You don't know how grateful we are," Jenny said.

"I am grateful to be of help," Greenfeather said. "It is not often these days that an old man is considered useful."

"You said two of your sons were with Waitie," Sweeney said. "What of the third?"

"Sweeney," Caitlin reprimanded. "Don't be rude."

"I'm curious," he said.

"My youngest son fights against everyone," Greenfeather said. "In addition to your war, there is another war here in the Cherokee Nation. It is an old feud, started by some of my old friends who came across before the removal. That is a nice word, is it not, for being marched away from your home at the point of a bayonet?"

"It is a word we understand," Sweeney said.

"Where are your friends?"

"Still outside," Trudy said.

"Then they are watching."

"Yes, I suppose they are."

"The Yankees are following you?"

Caitlin nodded.

"That explains it," the old Indian said. "I was surprised to find whites crossing this particular patch of land. It is an area that is generally avoided, and that is why I chose to make it my home—so that I would be left alone."

"Why is it avoided?" Jenny asked.

"Just old wives' tales," Sweeney said quickly.

"Let him talk," Jenny said. "I hope to be an old wife someday myself."

Greenfeather laughed.

"The Spanish called this area *camino diablo*— the Devil's Road, the Devil's Walk, something like that. My Spanish was never very good. The whites call it the Devil's Promenade."

"Spaniards?" Sweeney asked.

"Of course," Greenfeather said. "They had mines here, worked by our wild brothers from the southwest. Slaves."

"What kind of mines?" Caitlin asked.

"Lead, mostly, for their muskets. But this region is rich in minerals. There is also zinc, and crystal, and talc." Greenfeather went to the shelves, rummaged among them, and brought out a chunk of earthen-yellowed quartz crystal and a bit of white rock. He handed these to Caitlin.

"This is beautiful," Caitlin said, weighing the crystal in her hand. It was like a diamond the size of a hedge apple. "And this is so light." She handed the talc to Jenny.

"They make powder from that," Greenfeather said. "There was also talk that they found silver deep in the mines, but I do not believe it. There is always that kind of talk where you have mines."

"No reason to call this the devil's place," Sweeney said.

"Ah, that comes from the ghosts."

"Ghosts?" Caitlin asked, alarmed.

"Yes, from the slaves that worked the mines. Their spirits travel the hills here, balls of flame that float among the trees looking for their way home."

"I don't believe it," Sweeney said.

"There are other stories," Greenfeather said. "About lovers and soldiers and thieves. I'm not sure I believe in ghosts, either, but whatever it is, I have seen the lights often enough myself. Sometimes, I think, it is the Great Spirit wandering these hills."

Bone Heart could not sleep.

His left arm ached from the cold, and he was still wet from the river crossing, so he kept watch with his back against a tree and the Henry rifle in the crook of his undamaged right arm while the others slept. He had stripped out of his clothes—although there was no place to hang them to dry in the rain that continued to fall that night—and huddled beneath a yellow slicker.

His fingers probed the wound in his upper arm where the ramrod had entered as he stared into the darkness considering how close he had come to death. Sitting against the tree reminded him of the burial position of his people, the Little Ones, the Children of the Middle Waters. If he had fumbled a moment more with the rifle's mechanism, or if the enemy soldier's aim had been just slightly better, he would have been sleeping beneath the cold ground instead of feeling his bare buttocks against it—for the bluecoats would have hastily buried him according to their custom and then moved on.

But Wah'Kon-Tah, the Great Mystery, seemed to have other plans for him.

Bone Heart wished that it was later in winter so that the Dog Star, the life symbol of his people, would be above the horizon. It was the brightest star in the sky and it always made his heart sing, because it reminded him that each Osage is made half of the sky and half of the earth. But even if it were during the Time of the Moon When Trees Burst, he thought, this night would be too cloudy to see the Dog Star.

Bone Heart had not yet decided if Moonlight was a demon. He knew that the soldiers regarded his suspicion as the superstitious fancy of an unschooled savage, but he in turn was amazed at the white man's complete inability to glimpse the spirit world. The mysteries that surround life were so complex and so powerful that only a fool would ignore them; it would be, Bone Heart thought, like stumbling along a rocky path and refusing to open one's eyes.

14

Patrick woke.

Something was not right with Raven. The sound of shuffling hooves, a muffled protest, and the creak of leather brought him sharply around.

Patrick crept out of the cave and peered over the rocky bluff. It was dark, and still raining, but below he could see a couple of dark shapes moving around the horse.

"Don't try to ride him, Jay," a woman's voice whispered. "Jes' lead him away from here."

"Hell if I'm not," came the reply. "I'm tired of walking, and I don't see nobody around here to claim him."

One of the shapes swung up on Raven's back, and the horse reared.

Patrick cursed. He had a revolver in his hand, but he was afraid he would hit the horse if he risked a shot. So he slipped the revolver in his belt and tightened the buckle, drew his knife, and jumped.

He landed on the man's shoulder, knocked him from the horse, and they both went down in the mud at the woman's feet. Patrick was on top of the man and he laid the blade against his throat. The wind had been knocked out of the man, who could do little except cough.

"Indians!" the woman screamed.

"Shut up," Patrick said. "I'm no Indian, but I ought to cut his goddamned throat for trying to steal my horse."

"Didn't know it was your horse, mister," the man said.

"You knew it was somebody's," Patrick said.

"You already got me in the arm with that toad-sticker," the man said. "I'm bleeding pretty bad."

"Good," Patrick said.

"Let me up."

"No. You're liable to—"

The triple click of a revolver stopped him in mid-sentence.

The woman had a cocked dragoon held in both hands.

Patrick dropped the knife, rolled off the man, and pulled his own gun from his belt. The man sat up, holding his hands in front of him.

Sparks showered into the night as the dragoon roared.

The ball hit the man in the chest, driving him back into the mud, his mouth agape.

Patrick hesitated, his finger on the trigger. The woman was obscured by a cloud of black powder smoke. As the smoke drifted lazily away on the night breeze, he could see the woman still had the gun in front of her.

"You missed me," Patrick said, "and hit your man."

"I didn't like the bastard anyway," she said.

She cocked the gun again.

"If you don't put down that iron," Patrick said, "I'm going to have to kill you."

"Aileen?" the man called weakly amid a wet sucking sound.

"So kill me," she said. "Ain't nothin' to live for. Buried the young ones on the prairie in Missouri. He was the only kin I had left, and he beat me just like my pa did. Only, Pa never gave me a dose of syphilis."

She fired again.

This time the ball took off the top of his head.

"Bastard," she said.

"Put down the gun," Patrick said.

"Nope," the woman said as the smoke cleared.

She swung the barrel of the big dragoon over toward Patrick.

"There is no mercy in my heart," she said, and cocked the gun. "No mercy 'tall."

Patrick shot her in the left shoulder.

She fell backward, her dirty brown hair spilling around her, and landed with her arms outstretched. The dragoon, still clutched in her right hand, was driven into the mud.

"Damn," Patrick said.

Her eyes were open to the rain and her wet hair was plastered against her head.

"They're wrong," she said, and licked her lips. "It don't hurt to get shot. I don't feel a thing."

"You will soon enough," he said.

"How gallant," the woman said, more than a little crazily. "You winged me."

"I was trying to kill you," Patrick said. "But it's dark."

"It ain't easy to die, is it?" she asked. "Not as easy as in them books I read when I was a little girl. When a woman wanted to die of a broken heart, she just took to her bed and expired. I tried that, but it didn't work."

She pulled the gun from the mud and clutched it against her stomach.

"It's a little too easy to die, if you ask my opinion," Patrick said. "Quit with the gun already."

"I can't move my left arm."

"Your shoulder's busted."

"Come closer and help me."

Patrick stepped forward. When he was three feet away, she raised the gun in her right hand. The barrel danced in front of her and Patrick threw himself behind a tree.

The mud-filled dragoon exploded when she pulled the trigger.

The woman was still alive, but Patrick judged it was safe enough to come out from behind the tree. The gun was in pieces and the woman was missing three fingers from her right hand.

A chunk of iron the size of a marble had been blown from the cylinder and lodged in her forehead. Patrick could see the edge of the gnarled metal protruding from the wound. A trickle of blood pooled beside her nose. She was in convulsions, one of her eyes was filled with blood and the other was milky, and Patrick did not know if she could hear him or not.

"I'm sorry," he said.

He placed the barrel of his gun against her temple.

Bone Heart was the first to see the ruts of the wagon leading from the sandbar, and he called to Moonlight. The captain spurred Cerberus ahead of the sleepy troopers.

"What tiding sends my scout?" Moonlight asked gaily. "Prithee, speak!"

Bone Heart grunted and indicated the ground, unsure of precisely what Moonlight was asking.

Moonlight dismounted and studied the bar. Fog layered the river, shot with early-morning light. A heron waded on spindly legs at the head of the bar. A frog, startled by the approach of the horses, plopped into the water from a piece of driftwood. Beside the driftwood, an oar was stuck into the bar by its blade.

Moonlight walked over and snatched up the oar from where Botkins had driven it into the sand.

"Sir," Hendricks called. "There's a clear trail leading into the woods."

"Splendid," Moonlight called. He tossed the

oar aside and brushed the sand from his palms. "Before this day is over," he said, "the fight will be joined."

Annabel was asleep on Greenfeather's bed. She was breathing easier now, but Caitlin kept a watchful eye on her from a chair pulled up close.

"They will be coming," Frank said. "It may not be today, or the day after, but they will be here. The tracks lead up to the cabin, and you will be in great danger."

"Yes," Greenfeather said.

"Perhaps it would be wise to clear out for a few days," Frank said. "Let them pass. Come back when it is safe."

"There is nowhere else I want to go," Greenfeather said.

"There will be trouble."

"Yes."

"We must leave soon. You are welcome to come with us."

"No," Greenfeather said. "I will not leave my home. This is where I want to stay. When I die, I want to be buried out back with my wives."

"If you admit that you helped us," Frank said, "they are likely to shoot you. Tell them instead that we robbed you at gunpoint of food and medicine."

"I will not lie," Greenfeather said.

"It would not be too much of a lie," Frank said.

"That is what we had resolved to do in the first place. I am ashamed of what was in our hearts."

"Who would not do the same for their young ones?" Greenfeather asked, and smiled. "These decisions are the price of being a man, my son. There is nothing to forgive."

15

It was late in the afternoon when the squad rode up to the cabin. Greenfeather was sitting on the porch in a straight-backed chair, smoking his pipe.

The door to the cabin was open.

"Old man," Moonlight called from his horse. "Where is the wagon and the deserters?"

"I know nothing of deserters," Greenfeather said. "A family came to me in the middle of the night. Their baby was sick. They left a few hours ago."

"They were traveling in a military ambulance, no?"

"Yes, it was a curious-looking affair," Greenfeather said.

"The wagon was stolen and you have provided aid and comfort to the enemy," Moonlight said. "That is an offense punishable by death."

"Sir," Hendricks whispered. "We are no longer in Missouri. I'm not sure that martial law applies here. This is the Cherokee Nation."

"All is fair," Moonlight said. "We are still at war, are we not? Sergeant, search the cabin. Do it carefully, because these are cunning devils that we're after."

"You can see for yourself that the wagon left," Greenfeather said. "The tracks are plain enough."

"Step away from the cabin, old man."

Greenfeather refused.

"Bone Heart," Moonlight called. "Remove your educated cousin from the porch."

Bone Heart walked up on the porch and sneered. He grabbed Greenfeather by the collar with his good hand, pulled him out of the chair, and threw him onto the ground.

Greenfeather sat up and retrieved his pipe.

"So you now have Osage dogs doing your dirty work for you," Greenfeather said.

"Shut up!" Bone Heart barked. "The Cherokee are less than the dirt."

Bone Heart kicked the old man in the ribs.

The blow knocked the wind out of Greenfeather, and he lay on the cold winter ground, gasping for breath. When he could again sit upright, he said calmly:

"The Osage are a nation of cowards."

Bone Heart drew back his leg again, but Moonlight stopped him.

"That's enough," the captain said. "We don't want to hurt him so badly that he can't tell us where they've gone."

"You'll learn nothing from me," Greenfeather said.

"Sir!" the sergeant called. "Nobody else here. It appears they all left in the wagon."

"Thank you," Moonlight said. "Now, old man, what is your name?"

Greenfeather was silent.

"How many were there?"

Greenfeather looked away.

"How were they armed?"

The Cherokee said nothing.

"Very well," Moonlight replied to his silence, "It seems a little persuasion is needed here. Sergeant, douse the cabin with coal oil or whatever else you can find inside that will burn."

The sergeant nodded. He and a trooper each took a lamp from inside, removed the top, and sloshed kerosene over the inside of the cabin.

"Now, old man, if you don't want to be left homeless in the middle of winter, I suggest that you begin telling us what we want to know. How many were there?"

"I was once removed from my home in Georgia by soldiers like you," Greenfeather said. "I have thought of that many times over the years, and each time I am filled with anger and regret. You may burn my home, you may even beat me until death, but I will no longer submit."

"Hendricks, fire the cabin."

"Sir?"

"Get out your matches and set the cabin on fire," Moonlight said impatiently.

"No, sir," Hendricks said.

"I beg your pardon, Lieutenant?"

"Sir, it's wrong."

"This Indian is withholding information that is crucial to our mission," Moonlight fumed. "Time is short and we must use every means available to us."

"Respectfully, sir, he is a noncombatant," Hendricks said. "He has done us no harm. We cannot burn his home to the ground and leave him here to freeze to death in the middle of winter."

"Damn it all," Moonlight said. "Burn that cabin or you'll find yourself facing a court-martial when we get back to post."

"I refuse to comply with an unlawful order," Hendricks said. "Sir."

"Refuse?"

"I think it is you that should be brought up on charges."

"Hendricks, you are relieved of your duties," Moonlight said. "Join the enlisted men and consider yourself under arrest for the duration of our mission. If you attempt to escape, you will be shot. Is that understood?"

"Quite understood," Hendricks said.

"Your bars."

Hendricks ripped the patches from the shoulders of his uniform and handed them to Moonlight.

"If you make any more trouble for me," Moonlight said as he stuffed the insignia into his pocket, "if you so much as look at me the wrong way, I swear I will kill you myself and take pleasure in the act. I don't have time for this foolishness. Sergeant!"

The Sergeant who had been listening to the exchange from a prudent distance stepped forward.

"Yes, sir!"

"Burn the cabin."

"Very good, sir."

The sergeant stepped onto the porch of the cabin. He opened a box of matches, snapped one from the deck, and lit it. He cupped it in his hands for a moment, then tossed it through the doorway to the kerosene-soaked floor.

Patrick stood naked beside Raven and tied the bundle of clothes securely around the horse's neck, just above the saddle. In the middle of the bundle, wrapped in oilcloth, were his powder, caps, and loaded guns.

He swung up in the saddle. His bare feet felt strange in the stirrups. He guided Raven down the bank and into the river. It seemed shallower here, but there was no sure way to tell except by crossing. He patted Raven's neck and leaned down to whisper in the horse's ear.

"Just take it easy," he said.

Raven walked deeper into the river, the current tugging at his feet. When they were halfway across, the horse hesitated. The water was just touching Raven's belly.

The river swirled around Patrick's ankles. The cold made his legs ache.

"Come on," Patrick urged. "We may get lucky. Keep going."

Raven took a few more steps, and the water was up to Patrick's knees. He could feel Raven's shoes slipping on the moss-covered bottom, and suddenly Patrick was plunged underwater as Raven lost his footing and fell sideways into the deep river channel.

Patrick kicked free of the stirrups and came up, shaking water from his eyes. Raven was a few yards away, his head above water, swimming desperately.

Patrick kicked after him.

The current carried them fifty yards downstream before they could again find the bottom. Raven clattered up the rocky bank and Patrick followed on his hands and knees.

He called to the horse, but Raven backed away.

"Come here," Patrick said when he had caught his breath. "It's all right now."

Patrick grabbed Raven's bridle and pulled the horse to him. He draped his arms around his neck and said the kinds of things one would say to a frightened child.

Patrick loosened the bundle of clothes and threw it down on the bank. It was soaking. He undid the belt around it, took out the oilcloth from the center of the bundle, and examined the contents.

He thumbed the spout on the powder flask and shook it, but nothing but a dribble of water came out. He unscrewed the top of the flask and probed the contents with his finger. It was wet and clumped together like paste.

Patrick flicked the useless powder from the end of his finger and picked up a revolver. He cocked it, aimed at the base of a willow tree, and pulled the trigger.

The hammer fell on a dead chamber.

On the narrow trail that snaked through the dark hills, the wagon came to a stop. Caitlin eased herself to the ground, and Botkins handed down a crutch.

Frank turned Splitfoot and came up alongside.

"What's wrong?" he asked.

"I have to stop," Caitlin said, adjusting the crutch beneath her arm.

"What for?" Frank asked.

"I just have to," Caitlin hissed over her shoulder as she hopped into the woods.

"She has to answer the call of nature," Jenny said from the parted canvas. "She has been in agony for the last half hour, and she couldn't hold it anymore."

Frank looked anxiously at the trail behind them.

"What's wrong?" Botkins asked.

"We're being followed," Frank said.

"I have to go, too," Little Frank said, tugging at his mother's sleeve.

"Not now, honey," Jenny said. "In a little bit."

"I can't *wait*," he said.

"Take him," Frank said. "Then help Caitlin get back here just as quick as you can."

Jenny nodded and climbed down from the wagon with Little Frank on her hip.

"This is no good," Sweeney said, moving up in the wagon. "I've been watching from the tailgate. They've been staying about a hundred yards behind."

"Soldiers?" Frank asked.

"Yes," Sweeney said, "but it's hard to tell which side. Before the sun went down, all I could see was a bit of light blue trousers. That could mean anybody."

"Maybe it's not the Yankees," Trudy said hopefully.

"Whoever it is, it's not good," Frank said. "They want us to know they're back there. Trying to get us to run ourselves out before they close in."

"Or to catch us in the open," Sweeney said. "Where we can't make a fight of it."

"The fight's going to come quick enough," Frank said. "I hate this country. You can't see thirty yards clear in any direction. We need to have some sort of strategy to deal with it."

"So let them follow the wagon," Botkins said.

"That's what they're doing."

"No," Botkins said. "I mean, they would follow the wagon no matter if all of us were in it, or just one. The women are safer right now in the oods than they would be here in the wagon. For that matter, so would you."

"I can't let you go on alone."

"But what if we set up an ambush for them?" Sweeney asked. "Botkins here could take the wagon and drive like hell for a mile or two, until he comes to a likely spot—one with a steep cut on either side. We could set ourselves up on the high ground and they would have one helluva time getting out of there."

"There's too many of them," Frank said. "How many did you see back at the ferry? More than a dozen?"

"It beats the odds we're looking at now," Botkins said. "And the women and children would be away from the shooting."

"Let's pick our fight," Sweeney said, "instead of letting them pick it for us. But we have to do it now, before it gets any darker, or we won't be able to pick our terrain."

Frank rubbed his jaw with the back of his hand.

"All right," he said. "It's worth a try. Trudy?"

"I can fight," she said.

"No," Frank said. "I need you to take Ann
and go into the woods right now. Tell Caitlin
Jenny to stay put until the shooting is over."

"But I want—"

"No," Frank said. "I'm glad the others
already in the woods, so I don't have to ar
with each of you. Believe me, this is the o
way."

Trudy nodded.

"Botkins," Frank said. "You pick your sp
Sweeney and I will be right behind you, th
we'll double back and take up positions on eith
side of the road."

The blacksmith nodded.

Trudy handed Botkins her revolver. Then sh
wrapped Annabel in a blanket and dropped ove
the side to the ground.

"They are bolting, sir."

"What do you think, Sergeant?" Moonlight
asked. "Are they making a run for it, or are they
up to something?"

"I think we have them spooked, sir."

"Do we?" Moonlight asked. "The choice is to
give chase or to take our time. Prudence tells me
that we should take our time, but instinct tells
me that if we let them get a few miles ahead, they
will resort to trickery once again."

"It would be a shame to lose them now that we
are this close," the sergeant offered. "Shouldn't

ve press the matter and be done with it? We can't take the chance that they are putting some distance between us just so they can scatter like rabbits into the woods."

"Bone Heart," Moonlight said. "What is your pleasure?"

"Kill them now," the scout said, "before they hide."

"Sensible enough. All right, then. We shall overtake them and finish the matter once and for all. Sergeant, prepare the men for the offensive. On my command."

16

Caitlin dreaded answering nature's call. It had become a ritual ordeal that required a precise sense of balance, an ample amount of time, and a convenient tree to lean upon. Attempting the act in an unknown wood in the dark, and trying for completion as quickly as possible, further complicated matters.

The gunshots came while she was steadying herself against an oak tree and struggling back into her underthings. There were three or more pistol shots in quick order, followed by a thundering volley of rifles.

Caitlin was confused. The reports came not from the nearby road, but farther down, perhaps

as much as a mile. She had heard the sound of horses pass a few minutes earlier, but did not know what to make of it. Now she feared the worst.

After putting on her coat, she picked up the crutch and began to hobble back through the woods as quickly as her one leg would allow. She thought she was going back in the direction of the road, but after going a considerable distance, she had to admit to herself that she had become lost.

Caitlin paused. Although she was short of breath, she forced herself to control her breathing and listen. The gunshots continued, and she set a course by the sound.

A tree root snagged the end of the crutch, sending her cartwheeling down the hillside. Thorns ripped into her palms as she clawed frantically for a handhold, but she just kept moving faster as the angle of the slope increased. It was apparent that she was tumbling toward the bottom of a hole of some kind, but her momentum was so great that she could not stop her descent.

She slammed against a boulder and heard the sickening crack of ribs as she tottered for a moment over the lip of a rocky shelf. Her foot swung in space below her, and her fingernails clawed frantically against the face of the bare rock. She jammed the fingers of her right hand into a cleft in the rock.

She hung there, unable to find purchase for her other hand. There was a sharp pain in her side where she had hit the boulder, and the angle at which she was dangling from the rock made it increasingly difficult to breathe. A column of foul-tasting vomit rose in her throat.

Caitlin dared a glance over her shoulder.

The hole gaped like an open grave beneath her.

She called for help, but the pain in her ribs and shortness of breath prevented anything more than a few words at a time. The Lefaucheux revolver in her coat felt as if it were made of lead. She had slipped it into the pocket for protection before venturing into the woods, but now she wished she hadn't. Her arm was beginning to ache and she could no longer feel the fingers that were wedged into the rock.

"Help," she called, fighting for breath. "Frank! Anybody! I'm here. Help me. . . ."

There was no response, no comforting reassurance that she would soon be out. She was becoming dizzy, and she knew she could not hold on for much longer.

She looked down again at the hole.

It's dark, she thought. *Perhaps it's not as deep as it looks.*

With her left hand, she searched the pocket of her jacket for something she could toss into the hole. Her hand closed momentarily around the grip of the Lefaucheux, but she quickly rejected it and dug deeper. Eventually she found a thimble.

She held the thimble away from her body and dropped it.

If it struck the bottom, she did not hear it.

"Oh Lord," she said.

She closed her eyes and began to pray. She was still praying when her strength began to play out and she could feel her grip steadily loosen.

"Caitlin?"

She opened her eyes.

"My Lord, I thought I heard you calling."

Jenny was kneeling on the ledge of rock just above her.

"I can't hold on," Caitlin cried.

"Give me your other hand," Jenny said, leaning over the rock.

Caitlin raised her left arm and a knifing pain pierced her side. She grimaced, bit her lip, and forced her hand above her head.

Six inches remained between their fingertips.

"Just a little higher, honey."

"I can't," Caitlin wailed. "I'm going to fall."

"I'll have to get some help."

"Don't leave me!" Caitlin said. "You promised you wouldn't leave me. *Please.*"

Jenny leaned far out over the rock shelf.

Their fingers brushed.

Caitlin's teeth sliced through her lower lip and

blood streamed down her chin as she summoned the last of her strength to push her left hand higher. She could feel Jenny's fingers sliding over hers. Finally their palms met and Jenny's fingers closed over her hand.

Caitlin's strength failed.

She hung for a moment at the end of Jenny's grasp. Then they fell into the chasm together.

The squad charged down the road with Moonlight in the lead, their rifles at the ready. They slowed and bunched together as the road took a sharp cut between two hills, and as Moonlight emerged on the other side of the curve, he saw the dark shape of the wagon just ahead.

Moonlight gave a cry and spurred Cerberus forward.

Bone Heart fell back.

It was too late by the time Moonlight realized the wagon was unoccupied. The team had been unhitched. The tongue was lying across the road.

Cerberus slid on his haunches as Moonlight pulled back on the reins. He shouted for the squad to take cover, but his voice was lost amid the pistol fire that erupted from both sides of the cut.

Two troopers plummeted from their horses and a pistol ball nipped at the fabric of Moonlight's sleeve as he fought for control.

The soldiers returned fire, pumping shells through the Henrys as fast as they could work the levers, but they were shooting blindly into the dark hillsides. Another soldier fell in the road, struggled to his feet, and then was struck dead.

A wounded horse cried in agony.

"The rifles!" Moonlight screamed. "Get the rifles."

The sergeant jumped down from his horse while Moonlight peppered the spots on the hillside that had blazed with pistol fire moments before. There seemed to be at least two snipers on the eastern slope and another to the west, but he could not be sure.

The sergeant gathered up a pair of Henrys, but he could not find the third. When a bullet chipped the stock of one of the rifles beneath his arm, he gave up the search.

Moonlight retreated with what remained of the squad.

At first Jenny did not know whether she was alive or dead. Although her eyes were open, they saw nothing—she was enveloped by utter darkness, a darkness she had never known was possible.

"Caitlin?"

"I'm here."

"Are you hurt badly?"

"Badly enough. I can't really tell."

"Where are we?"

"Some kind of mine shaft, I reckon. Are you in one piece?"

"Bruised, but not broken."

"Do you hear anything?"

"Water. I hear the sound of water dripping, but that's all."

"The shooting has stopped?"

"Yes, some time ago."

"What was it?"

"I don't know, Cait. I didn't have a chance to find out."

"Where's Little Frank?"

"Up above. I told him to wait for me while I went down for you. Do you have any matches, or a candle . . . ?"

"No."

"Well, at least it's warm down here. It *is* warmer, don't you think?"

"We're closer to hell."

"The earth stays warmer in winter and cooler in summer. You're no closer to hell than you were an hour ago."

"I knew that."

"We should be able to see the stars, though. Where are the stars?"

"We rolled down a muddy slope of some kind after we fell. I'm so turned around, Jenny, that I can scarcely tell which way is up."

"Frank!" Jenny called. "Little Frank!"

"Don't," Caitlin said. "He will trip in the darkness and fall into the hole with us."

"We must find a way out."

"Please," Caitlin said. "Let me rest first. I haven't the strength to move an inch. Stay with me while I rest . . . stay with me a spell."

17

Little Frank crouched in the darkness and hugged his knees to his chest, waiting for his mother to return. Although he was not frightened, he did not like the deep woods, and the sound of nearby gunfire was disturbing. He tried to think of things he enjoyed—his bag of marbles back in the wagon, the songs that Trudy sang to him, his mother's milk—but the sound of the gunfire was too intense for him to dwell upon these things for long. When the shooting finally stopped, the silence that followed was even more disturbing.

He thought he heard his mother's voice call his name. It sounded weak and very far away.

"Mama?" he called.

Little Frank stood. He turned in a slow circle as he looked around him. The woods appeared to be the same in every direction.

"Mama?" he called again, louder now.

He had never been left alone for so long. His lower lip began to tremble.

"Mama!"

Tears covered his cheeks. He rubbed his eyes with his fists, fighting the very reasonable fear of being separated from his mother in this strange place. Then he began to ponder the possibility of never seeing her again—although it had been less than half an hour, to Little Frank it was the same as an eternity.

He sat down on the ground and began to sob in earnest.

When he had no more tears left, he slumped as if in a stupor, his chin on his chest, his entire being throbbing with loneliness. Where were the others? Trudy or Aunt Caitlin had always been near at hand before. Where could they have gone?

Then something caught his eye, far away through the woods. It was a light, moving slowly, seeming to wink on and off as trees interfered with his line of sight.

He stood to get a better look at it.

The hazy ball of light continued to bob and weave.

It has to be the wagon, Little Frank thought. His mother and the others would be there—their world had centered upon the wagon now for what seemed like forever—and they must be searching for him. Perhaps they were using a lantern so that he could see where they were, so that he could find them in the darkness.

He hurried through the woods toward the light.

His feet seemed to pick their own way around stumps and over rocks, and the closer he got to the light, the better he felt. When he reached the road he did not think it strange that the light was still far on the other side.

Trudy, who was standing beside the road with Annabel in her arms, saw him emerge from the woods. He did not pause, but walked straight across the road toward the other side.

"Little Frank," she called. "Stop."

He stopped and waited impatiently for Trudy to catch up. The light seemed to be moving faster now, and he was afraid that he would lose it.

Trudy hurried over the twenty yards that separated them. She knelt and clutched the boy's hand.

"Where's your mother?" she asked.

"In the wagon," he said confidently.

"No," Trudy said. "She can't be. . . ."

"Look," he said, and pointed at the light.

"What in the world?" Trudy asked.

It was unlike anything she had seen before. Instead of the orange glow of a lantern, or the reddish light cast by a fire, the light radiated a cool bluish-white color.

"Let's go," Little Frank said, his hand slipping from hers.

"Wait," she said.

Instead of hesitating, the boy continued his scramble toward the light with renewed vigor.

Trudy plunged into the woods after him,

clutching Annabel between her breasts with both hands, being careful of where she placed her feet lest she trip.

There was a peculiar scent on the breeze, a clean smell, one that she normally associated with clear flowing water. But there was no stream nearby, and the closer she got to the light, the more unnerved she became.

Her breath came in spasms and her nostrils flared. Then she topped a small rise and found Little Frank on his knees on a carpet of dead leaves on the other side of the slope, clapping his hands with joy as he watched the antics of the glowing ball of bluish fire not thirty yards away.

The light appeared to dance, to wobble, to drift up to the tops of the trees and then float lazily back down. It glowed brightly enough that she could make out the pattern in the bark of the trees behind it, and count the individual leaves on the ground below.

"What is it?" Trudy asked.

"It's an angel," Little Frank said matter-of-factly.

Trudy fell to her knees beside the child.

"I see it," she said.

Annabel looked sleepily at the glowing sphere, then glanced away, unimpressed. The light darted, circled around an oak, and came back toward them.

Trudy removed her coat and lay Annabel on it, next to Little Frank, and tucked the blanket around her feet. The baby kicked away the blanket and wiggled her toes contentedly.

Trudy clasped her hands together beneath her chin.

"I see it," she said.

Tears came to her eyes.

"My God, I see it."

The light flared so brightly that she was afraid the woods would burst into flame. She was afraid and excited at the same time. She thought of the story of Moses and the burning bush, and she tried to pray, but abandoned the effort because she was afraid that she would not do it correctly.

Was this God? Jehovah? Or was it Wah'Kon-Tah, the Great Mystery?

The brilliant light burst into a trio of smaller lights—one red, one blue, one green—and they swirled together in a glowing helix rising above the ground. Then the night wind stirred and the trinity was carried away over the tops of the trees, leaving the woods once again in darkness.

"It's gone," Little Frank said sadly.

He stood up and brushed the leaves from his clothes.

Trudy could not speak or move. She swept up Annabel and held her tightly against her, then drew Little Frank to her as well. The boy endured the embrace for several moments, then squirmed and slipped away.

"Let's go find Mama," he said.

18

Caitlin?"

"I'm awake."

"We need to get out of here."

"I've been thinking," Caitlin said. "Perhaps there is a way that we can get a little light. Can you tear some strips of cloth from your undergarments?"

Caitlin took the revolver from her coat pocket and fumbled with the cylinder. Finally she managed to open it, and she extracted one of the cartridges. She put the tip of the cartridge in her mouth, gripped the lead bullet with her teeth, and twisted it loose from the casing.

"Let me have some cloth," she said.

Caitlin found Jenny's elbow, then followed her arm to her hand and took the cloth. She tore a small piece from the end of the strip, wadded it loosely, and stuffed it into the end of the bullet.

She replaced the bullet in the cylinder and, using her fingers for eyes, carefully turned it until it was next in line to fire. Then she put the rest of the cloth in a pile and placed the barrel of the revolver in it.

"What are you doing with the gun?" Jenny asked when she heard the sound of the hammer being cocked.

"I'm trying to light a fire," Caitlin said. "Scoot away and turn your head. I don't know how safely I can do this."

Caitlin pulled the trigger and the Lefaucheux popped, sending a shower of burning powder into the cloth. The cloth smoked and burst into flame.

"Good work," Jenny said admiringly. "I would never have thought of it."

"Quickly," Caitlin said. "You need to find some sticks, wood, anything that will burn. Once we have a fire going, we can take our time poking around. What's wrong?"

"Nothing," Jenny said. Caitlin's face was bruised, tight with pain, and smeared with dried blood. Jenny looked away.

The tunnel was round, and the walls and ceiling were shored every so often with rough pieces of very old-looking timber. The floor was littered with thousands of flint chips, so white and fragile that it brought an image to Jenny's mind of a team of madmen smashing crates of china on rocks with sledgehammers.

One end of the tunnel ended in darkness, and it appeared to go far back into the hillside. The other stopped abruptly in a pile of debris. The ceiling had caved in unknown years ago, creating the sinkhole into which they had fallen.

Jenny gathered some scattered pieces of timber from the floor and carefully fed them to the fire.

Caitlin reached behind her, grimacing with

pain, and searched the ground with her hand. It hurt too much to turn her head and look. Her fingers closed over some sticks, and she pulled them to her. They seemed to be gathered in some sort of decaying fabric, and she tossed the bundle into the fire. She reached back for more, found another stick, and pulled.

The movement dislodged something that rolled across the floor.

Caitlin glanced down at the stick in her hand before tossing it into the fire, and realized it wasn't a stick at all.

It was a bone.

The thing that had rolled toward her was a lopsided human skull, and it lay staring at her with empty sockets a few inches from where she sat.

Jenny looked over and stifled a scream.

"It's all right," Caitlin said, and calmly placed the arm bone down. "It can't do us any harm."

"Apparently we're not the first visitors here," Jenny said.

"As long as we're just visiting," Caitlin said, "and don't become permanent residents like this fellow here."

Jenny began to laugh.

"It wasn't that funny," Caitlin said.

"If I don't laugh," Jenny said, "I'll cry."

"Put his head back, will you?"

Jenny nodded.

She gingerly picked up the skull and the arm bone and placed them in their relative positions with the rest of the skeleton. Caitlin could see that one side of the skull had been badly crushed.

"Who do you suppose he was?" Caitlin asked.

"He died a long time ago," Jenny said. "There's some leather here, and some bits of rusted metal. Maybe Greenfeather was right. This is a mine of some sort. Perhaps he was Spanish."

"Or Indian," Caitlin said.

"No. Look at this."

Jenny picked up a badly deteriorated sword. The blade was all but eaten away, but the handle—which was tarnished a deep green color—was still complete.

"Do you think an Indian might have bashed in his skull?"

"An Indian would have taken the sword," Caitlin said. "No, I think he probably just stumbled and fell, just like we did—although we were a mite luckier."

Jenny laid the sword at the skeleton's side and brushed her hands. Then she took a piece of flaming wood from the fire.

"We must have rolled down this incline," Jenny said. "The ground's been sloughing off into this hole for years. I'm going to see if we can climb out."

With the torch in front of her, Jenny inched her way up the mound. She was gone for a minute or so, and when she returned she was covered with mud and clay.

"You're not afraid of snakes, are you?" Jenny asked as she laid the end of the torch back into the fire.

"No," Caitlin said.

"Well, I am," Jenny said. "And they're thick as ticks up there. Copperheads. They appear to be asleep, but I don't think we can climb over them without getting bitten. Besides, the hole is too deep to get out without a rope."

"I don't think I'm going to get out at all," Caitlin said. She was sitting against the wall, her foot propped in front of her, her skirt covering her leg.

"Of course you will," Jenny said. "We both will. We haven't explored the rest of the tunnel. There could be an easy way out, just waiting for us to find it."

"You don't understand," Caitlin said. "I broke your fall when we tumbled down the shaft. While you were gone, I summoned up the courage to take a look at myself."

She lifted the skirt from her lower leg.

The bones above her ankle were twisted and bulged beneath the bruised skin at an unnatural angle.

"My leg is broken," Caitlin said. "And my ribs hurt so badly that I can hardly breathe, much less crawl."

Jenny knelt beside Caitlin and touched her face. Caitlin began to weep.

"Don't leave me here," Caitlin said. "I know I should tell you to save yourself, to get out and find the others, but I'm terrified. I'm afraid to die, Jenny. I don't want to live anymore, but I'm afraid to die."

"So am I," Jenny said, cradling Caitlin's head in her arms. "But we can't give up. I'm going to explore the other end of the tunnel."

"Don't leave me."

"I must, but just for a little while," Jenny said. "I'll be back. Remember, I'm not going anywhere without you."

Moonlight, his scout Bonc Hcart, and the five surviving members of the squad bivouacked in a clearing by a stream a few miles up the road from whcrc thc fight had takcn placc.

The numbers were beginning to alarm Moonlight. The repeating rifles had inspired a false sense of confidence, and superior tactics had proved their worth. He was even concerned that the deserters might track them down and finish them while they slept, so he ordered no fires. At least two troopers were to be on guard at any time, and the remainder were to sleep fully outfitted with their weapons by the sides.

Moonlight sat on his haunches and traced a long line in the dirt with a stick, attempting to formulate a plan. The line stood for the road, and a circle for their camp. The place where the fight had taken place was represented by a pair of angry, slashing lines. A wavy line, far below the others, was the North Canadian River—the Confederate line.

The sergeant stood over Moonlight and placed his boot in the middle of Moonlight's map.

"Begging the captain's pardon," the sergeant said, "but you're a fool."

"I don't remember giving you permission to speak your mind," Moonlight said.

"I'm speaking the truth," the sergeant said.

"All right," Moonlight said. He took a cigar from his vest pocket, bit the end from it, and lit it. "You may have your say."

"That was a shavetail thing you did this afternoon. The ambush could have been predicted. And then you compounded the problem by running. We should have regrouped and flanked them. There were three of them, sir, just three. There were ten of us."

"You had better be thankful we're out of earshot of the men, Sergeant," Moonlight said. "Otherwise, I wouldn't be able to ignore your insubordination."

"Dammit," the sergeant said. "Can't you even call me by name or look me in the face? My name is O'Reilly, sir. And I have spent a lifetime in this man's army, long before the war came and brought amateurs like you crawling out of the woodwork."

"May I remind you of my record of enemy kills?"

"You're not an officer, you're not even a soldier; you're an assassin. You prefer to slip up on the enemy and do your killing in the dark, using that damned Indian like some kind of bird dog. You won't stand and fight like a man. Oh, you're bold enough when you're torturing some poor old Indian to death. But now that you've run up against some men with sand, you're scared, and it shows."

"That's enough, Sergeant," Moonlight said.

"Quite enough, sir," O'Reilly said. "When we get back to post, I intend to ask for reassignment. I respect your uniform enough to keep the reasons to myself, but between us, you're not worth the spit of the men you're chasing."

Botkins hitched the team and pulled the wagon off the road and into the woods. Then he began to dig a trio of shallow graves in the rocky soil.

Sweeney found the Henry rifle on the road beside one of the corpses. He discovered thirty rounds for the repeating rifle in the pockets of the soldier, and another dozen unfired cartridges mixed among the spent shells littering the road.

"Some of them must have been so scared they weren't even pulling the trigger," Sweeney said.

165

"They were just levering shells through the action."

Frank put one of the dead men across his shoulders and dumped him unceremoniously on the ground next to where Botkins was shoveling dirt and rock.

"Why should we have to bury 'em?" Botkins asked. "I don't reckon it's any of our business."

"It's the decent thing to do," Frank said. "Besides, we're not going anywhere until the women catch up with us. What do you think could be taking them so long?"

"Maybe the Yankees have them," Botkins said, rolling the corpse over into the first of the graves.

"No," Frank said. "We would have heard from them by now. They would have wanted to negotiate, to trade their freedom in exchange for us."

Botkins shook his head and began to fill the grave.

Frank returned to the road and found Sweeney eyeing a gold tooth in the mouth of one of the corpses.

"Tell me you're not that depraved," Frank said.

"I'll tell you anything you want."

"Then tell me you'll give me a hand," Frank said.

Sweeney had abandoned the dental work to its owner, but was now going through the soldier's pockets. On the ground beside him he had placed a pocket watch, a knife, and a small wad of greenbacks and assorted coins.

"Just a minute," Sweeney said.

"Let the dead be," Frank said.

"They weren't going to let us be, were they?" Sweeney asked moodily as he stuffed the loot into his own pockets.

Frank grasped the boots of another soldier while Sweeney got him beneath the arms. They lifted the man between them and he gave a low, nearly inaudible moan.

"This one ain't dead," Sweeney said.

They put him back down and Frank knelt beside him. There was a dark stain on his tunic from a stomach wound. Frank undid his belt and examined the wound with a grim face. His hands came away covered with fresh blood.

"He won't make it long," he said.

The man's eyes fluttered open.

"Can you hear me?" Frank asked.

The soldier nodded.

"I'm dying," he said.

Frank nodded.

"What's your name?"

The man licked his lips.

"Do you have any water?"

Sweeney brought a canteen from the wagon. Frank uncapped the canteen, placed his hand behind the man's head, and poured some water into his mouth. He managed to swallow a little, but most of the water dribbled down his chin.

"Thank you," the man said. "Hendricks. My name is Hendricks. Are you the deserters?"

"I reckon we are," Frank said. "Do you have the women?"

"The women?"

"Our women," Frank said. "And children."

"No," Hendricks said. "We found no women on the road."

"Damn," Sweeney said. "I wonder where they are."

"We're staying here until we find out," Frank said.

"Moonlight won't be back for a spell," Hendricks said. "I saw his face. You scared the living hell out of him."

"Moonlight?"

"Captain Moonlight," Hendricks said. "That's who is chasing you. He's got his orders, direct from General Blunt, to bring you in dead."

"Can I do anything for you?" Frank asked.

"My wife," Hendricks said. "Our home is in Iowa. The address is here, in my pocket. Would you be good enough to write her for me?"

"Yes," Frank said.

He took the paper from the man's pocket.

"What do you want me to say?"

"Tell her that I love her," Hendricks said, "and that my last thoughts flew to her and our baby."

"I will."

"Tell her not to mourn too much, that I wish her happiness and a full life. Tell her I died with honor, despite losing my bars. Moonlight is a madman, you know."

"Don't talk so much," Frank said.

"I've read that one is supposed to be filled with peace when the hour of one's death is at hand," Hendricks said. "It is strange, but I feel only anger. Rage."

Hendricks began to cough. When he recovered somewhat, he looked into Frank's eyes. He struggled again to speak, but could not form the words. He wanted to tell him to kill Moonlight when the opportunity again arose, to kill him while reminding him of the young lieutenant whose hatred would not die.

"Kill," was all Hendricks could get out before he died.

The sun was coming up as Frank and Sweeney laid the last of the soldiers into the grave. Botkins began to throw shovelfuls of dirt over the body, and Sweeney tossed some rocks on for good measure.

"Reckon we ought to say something?" Botkins asked.

"Good riddance," Sweeney said. "Dead Yankees fill my heart with joy."

"And your pockets with silver," Frank added.

"The Lord giveth," Sweeney said.

"Sometimes He does," Frank said, and picked up the Henry rifle from where it leaned against the side of the wagon. He retrieved the box of shells and began slipping them into the tubular magazine beneath the barrel.

"Do you mind?" Frank asked.

"Take it," Sweeney said. "It ain't my style."

Trudy appeared, carrying Annabel and leading Little Frank by the hand. The boy called out and ran to his father, who put the rifle down and swept him up.

"I heard the shooting," Trudy said tiredly. "Was there much trouble?"

"For them," Frank said, indicating the graves. "We're safe enough for now, I think."

"Where's Jenny and Cait?"

"I don't know," Trudy said. "I was hoping they were with you. Little Frank thought Jenny was with the wagon, then told me that she had gone to help Caitlin, who was in some kind of trouble. Fell into some kind of hole."

Trudy did not have to ask about Patrick. It was obvious that there was no sign of him, either. She thought of telling Frank about the light she had seen in the woods, but she did not have the words to describe it. Had she seen a ghost? Or an angel, as Little Frank suggested? Or was it the very spirit of God, beckoning her toward some fate that had yet to be revealed?

• • •

Jenny proceeded cautiously down the tunnel, the flame held well in front of her, afraid that anything she might touch would cause a cave-in.

The corridor led deep into the hillside. Her aging piece of wood made for a poor torch, because it was burning hot and fast. Before she was gone five minutes, the flame had consumed more than half the wood. She paused, found another discarded piece of timber on the ground, and lit it with the flame from the first.

Then she pressed onward.

The tunnel seemed to go on forever.

She was ready to give up and return to Caitlin when her flame dislodged a family of bats from the ceiling of the tunnel, and they flapped madly about her. Jenny crouched on the ground and covered her head with her arm, lest the flying rodents become entangled in her hair. Finally the bats left, racing down the tunnel toward an unseen destination.

She followed the bats.

The tunnel suddenly opened into a wide natural cavern. Her makeshift torch did not throw light far enough to see things clearly, but a still pool of water lay across most of the floor. She walked to the edge of the water and attempted to gauge its depth, but there was no way to tell without wading into it. She took a stone and threw it overhand as far as she could.

The splash was disquieting in the stillness.

Jenny lowered the flame and put her left hand in front of it to hide its glare. Across the water, high up on the far side, a shaft of sunlight pierced the darkness.

19

Jenny grasped Caitlin's ankle and pulled.

Caitlin clenched her teeth. Perspiration beaded on her forehead and her fingers clawed at the ground. When the pain became unbearable, she let out a shriek that echoed throughout the mine.

"Stop," Caitlin said. "No more. I can't stand it."

"We must do this," Jenny said. "If we don't set them, I'm afraid the bones will tear through the skin while I carry you out of here."

"Let them," Caitlin gasped.

"Then you will be a cripple for the rest of your life," Jenny said. "Here, put this in your mouth and bite down on it. You're going to have to help me by pulling in the other direction."

Jenny placed a stick between Caitlin's teeth.

She pulled again, putting all her strength into her right shoulder and hand while manipulating the break with her left. She could feel the ends of the bones grate together.

Caitlin threw her head back and fiercely bit

down on the stick. She growled and moaned like a muzzled beast caught in a trap, and leaned back on her elbows despite every instinct to relieve the pressure.

Jenny felt the tibia, the larger of the two bones, lock into place beneath her thumb. The fibula seemed to be appropriately positioned as well. Jenny released the pressure. Caitlin's foot now seemed to rest at a normal angle, although the ankle was badly bruised and swollen.

Caitlin spat the stick from her mouth.

"You could have wiped it clean first," she said, spitting. "It was covered with dirt and God knows what all."

"I tried, but it's dark," Jenny said. "How does your leg feel now?"

"It hurts like the devil," Caitlin said. "What do you think it would feel like?"

"And this?" Jenny asked, pinching her little toe.

"That hurts, too," she said. "Will you stop poking at me?"

Jenny smiled. She took the stick Caitlin had used, and another two like it, tying them tightly around Caitlin's lower leg with strips of cloth.

"That's the best we can do for now," Jenny said.

"Where did you learn to do that?" Caitlin asked.

"I've read about it," Jenny said. "In medical books."

"Books," Caitlin snorted. "I should have known. It's a good thing you didn't read a veterinary manual."

"Judging by your tongue, I'd say you're well enough to be moved," Jenny said. "Put your arms around my neck. There, that's it."

Caitlin sucked in her breath. The pain in her ribs was like a white-hot poker.

"Am I as light as a child?" Caitlin asked when she was up on Jenny's back.

"Not quite," Jenny said, straining. She locked her hands beneath Caitlin's thighs.

"You're supposed to tell me I am," Caitlin said deliriously. "At least, that's what the men do when they pick up the heroines in those silly stories."

"You're going to have to hold on tight," Jenny said, "and quit talking so much. You're also going to have to carry the torch so we can see where we're going."

Jenny leaned down and grabbed a piece of timber from the fire. As she did, Caitlin's foot scraped the ground.

"Dammit," Caitlin said.

"Sorry."

"That hurts. Would you watch what you're doing?"

"I'm trying," Jenny said. "Here we go. Watch your head, because the ceiling is quite low in places, and there are bats."

"Bats?"

"And get the torch out of my face, would you? You almost set my hair on fire."

They set off awkwardly down the tunnel.

Jenny had to set Caitlin down three times before they reached the cavern. At the edge of the pool of water, they rested. The patch of daylight on the other side of the cavern had grown brighter.

"We're going to have to leave our coats here," Jenny said. "We don't know how deep this is going to be, and the lighter we are, the better."

Caitlin took the revolver out of her coat before folding it and laying it upon the bank.

"Leave it here," Jenny said.

"No," Caitlin said, holding the gun defensively.

Jenny picked Caitlin up again, and they abandoned the torch, which had burned down too far to be of use. Jenny waded out into the pool, and when the water came up to her knees, she became more cautious, testing the depth of the water before each step. The water was like ice, and in a few minutes Jenny began to lose feeling in her feet.

With the water up to her waist, she stumbled, and nearly dropped Caitlin before regaining her balance. She leaned over until her nose almost touched the water as Caitlin centered herself again.

"It's all right," Caitlin said, encouraged now by the nearness of the daylight. "Just take your time."

After a few more steps Jenny stopped.

"It's getting too deep," she said.

"Can you swim?"

"Of course I can swim. But you can't.

"I can float, I think," Caitlin said. "At least, I used to be able to, when we swam in the river as kids. There's less of me now, so I should float better, shouldn't I? Let me go."

"No. You'll drown."

"We'll both drown if you don't," Caitlin said. "Let me go."

"Drop the gun," Jenny said.

Caitlin released the hold on the Lefaucheux and it slipped into the water.

Jenny eased Caitlin down.

Caitlin slid off and her head went under, then came back up. She took a deep breath, held it, and straightened her back and put out her arms.

"There," she said, blowing water away from her mouth.

Jenny reached into the water and struggled with her shoes, cursing the laces. Finally she managed to loosen them and kick them off.

"All right," Jenny said. "Here we go."

She waded out into the water, pulling Caitlin like a raft behind her, her toes barely touching the bottom. Then there was no bottom, and she kicked out. She turned in the water and grasped Caitlin around the shoulders.

"Relax," she said.

"Cold," Caitlin said.

"I know. You're doing fine."

Caitlin tried to say something else, but got a mouthful of water. She gagged, and water sprayed from her mouth and nose.

Jenny kicked with both feet and used her right arm in short strokes, and slowly they made their way across the deepest part of the pool. After ten yards Jenny could again touch the bottom. With long steps she struggled up the bank, pulling Caitlin behind her.

Caitlin lay shivering and coughing.

"Are you all right?"

"I'm freezing," Caitlin said. "We're still trapped in an abandoned mine. I have one leg, and it's busted, and what feels like a side full of broken ribs. Other than that, I'm just fine."

20

Patrick knelt amid the ashes of the cabin, poking about with a stick. Despite the rain, there were still some embers on the underside of the largest timber.

There was also evidence of a wagon and many horses in the yard, and boot prints all around the cabin. Despite the rain, there was enough left of the tracks that Patrick had some idea of the sequence of events.

What bothered him most, however, was the fresh grave out back.

It was unmarked.

Patrick stood, brushing the ashes from his hands. He called to Raven, and the horse walked over. Patrick gathered the reins and put his foot in the stirrup.

"Hold it."

A pair of men had ridden into the clearing, and one of them had a sawed-off shotgun pointed in Patrick's direction.

"What's your name?" the man with the shotgun asked.

"That depends upon who's asking," Patrick said, his foot still in the stirrup.

"*I'm* asking, and that's all you need to know."

"All right. My name is Patrick Fenn. Can I put my foot down now?"

"Do it slow. What do you know about this cabin?"

"Nothing," Patrick said. "I just rode up a little while ago. Found it just like this. Don't even know who lived there."

"Our father lived there," the man with the shotgun said. "We buried him yesterday. Figured it was border raiders that done this."

"It wasn't," Patrick said.

"I thought you said you don't know nothing about it," the one with the shotgun said, leaning forward in his saddle.

"I don't," Patrick said, "except for what I can see in the tracks. The rain's washed most of them away, but from what's left you can tell it was Union soldiers. Look at how well their horses were shod. All the nails in place. Guerrillas are generally short on nails, so they don't use but three on each shoe."

"Maybe."

"They also left a lot of fancy trash behind. Sardine tins and canned oysters. Did your father ever eat that well?"

"Guerrillas do, when they can steal it," the man with the shotgun said. "Maybe the Yankees were chasing the guerrillas that done this."

"And left your father to rot? If they had time to eat supper, they had time to bury him."

"He makes sense, Luke," the other one said.

"Shut up, Langston. I don't like him," Luke said, still holding the shotgun on Patrick. "He looks like the kind of trash that would do this, and story about it later. And if he didn't do it, I'm sure he's done just as worse up in Kansas."

"You're right, I have," Patrick said. "I helped Quantrill burn Lawrence to the ground. I shot more than my share of Blunt's troopers at Baxter Springs. And I've lost count of the widows and orphans I've made. But I didn't do this."

Patrick put his foot back in the stirrup and swung up in the saddle. His coat fell back, revealing the butt of a revolver.

"I'm sorry about your pa," Patrick said, "but if you don't throw that scattergun down, I'm going to have to kill both of you. I won't have you shooting me in the back while I ride away, just so you can satisfy your wrongheaded need for revenge."

"Why, you sonuva—"

Before Luke could thumb the hammers back on the shotgun, Patrick had his revolver out, cocked, and pointed at the man's chest.

"Throw it down, Luke," Langston said. He already had his own pistol out, and he tossed it to the ground. "He means it. Give it up."

Luke blinked. The barrel of the shotgun wilted downward.

"To the ground," Patrick said.

Luke lowered the shotgun until the butt touched the ground, then let it fall sideways to the wet grass.

"That's better," Patrick said.

Patrick nudged Raven into an easy walk. He replaced the useless pistol in his belt. He had nearly made it to the edge of the clearing when Langston Greenfeather called after him.

Jenny crawled up the rock-lined wall of the cavern to the sunlight and attempted to squeeze her shoulders into the opening that led to the outside. She could get one shoulder in, but not both, because the crevice was too narrow.

She reached her arm through the opening, feeling the daylight on her skin, and attempted to dislodge some of the boulders from around the opening. But it was no use. The rocks were too heavy and she could not get the leverage she needed with her arm fully extended.

"Damn," she said, enraged.

Jenny thrust her hand again through the opening, harder this time, the rocks cutting into her hand and wrist as she pushed with all of her might.

"Watch your language," Caitlin called from where she lay on the floor of the cavern. "We've come this far, and we don't want to tempt God to leave us here."

"I've about had it with that mean old bastard," Jenny said.

"Jenny, don't. You've picked up some mighty bad habits from that family you married into."

"I mean it," Jenny said. "We've come this far and we deserve some help. Are You listening to me, You fat Old Testament sonuvabitch? Haven't You caused enough death and pain and war already? Give me the strength of ten if You're up there. Show us some of Your mercy. I admit I'm afraid of dying and I'm afraid of You! Isn't that what You want? Help us!"

Jenny drew her hand back and wept.

"Why don't you try praying?" Caitlin asked.

"I *was* praying," Jenny said.

• • •

Bone Heart had left the camp before first light to seek out a hill upon which to talk to his creator. His heart was troubled and he needed guidance.

He was certain now that Moonlight was insane. He was not a demon, as he had feared, but just another crazy white man. War was given to the People as a noble experience, one that was supposed to lift the heart and elevate both victor and vanquished. Respect was required. But Bone Heart had learned that there was no respect in the way the whites made war. Where were the speeches and the gestures that made war meaningful? Nowhere. What provisions did they make for the women and children of those who were slain? None. Moonlight's lodge should be full of adopted wives and children, but he was alone.

Bone Heart found a rocky hillside, put his rifle down, and stripped to his breechclout. He sat cross-legged, facing the east, and watched the sun rise. He remained motionless for hours, until he heard the cry of a woman.

At first he didn't know what to make of the sound, for it seemed to come from inside the hill itself. The earth was crying, he thought. Or perhaps it was the little people the Cherokee spoke of that lived in the earth. Then he spotted the white hand thrusting up through the rocks below him.

He hurried down the hillside and inspected the

fissure from which the hand had come. As he sat on his heels peering into the darkness, he could plainly hear the conversation of human beings, of white women, trapped within the earth. He laboriously began to move aside the rocks, favoring his wounded arm.

A woman came to the opening and he grasped her hand. There was just enough room for her to get through the widened space, and he pulled her to him.

She was covered with mud and her clothes were wet and clung to her. She stood unsteadily for a moment, letting the sun shine on her face, mouthing a prayer of thanks. Then she reached to embrace him, and he instinctively pulled back. She grasped his hand instead and held it.

He stared at her figure, pausing on the places where the wet clothes clung to her breasts and hips. He was curious, because he had never been able to inspect a white woman in such detail before. They seemed not yet fully formed, Bone Heart thought, with narrow hips that were unsuited for childbirth; they also smelled, like all whites, of the greasy food they ate. No wonder the white men seemed constantly discontented.

Jenny stared at his body as well. His skin was the same bronze color all over, and he had no hair except for the stiff bristle that crested his skull. His genitals were tied in some curious fashion in a leather pouch.

She turned away, embarrassed at her own curiosity.

"What a naked devil you are," she said. "And what a sight I must seem to you. I do hope you don't get ideas. I am thankful, but decidedly not that thankful."

Bone Heart said nothing.

"My husband is not far away," she added.

"The other," Bone Heart said.

"Of course," Jenny said. "There is another. We must get her out. Can you carry her?"

Bone Heart nodded.

"She is injured. Her leg and ribs are broken. She has only one leg, so please be careful. You do understand me, don't you?"

"She is hurt," Bone Heart said, careful to speak correctly. "Many among us speak English for a long time now. Bone Heart speaks well when he wants, no?"

"Very well," Jenny said.

"Only, I don't want to all the time," he said. "It makes white men angry. No whites speak Osage, though, just a few squaw men. Very rude."

"Yes, I suppose it is."

He widened the hole a bit more so that he could squeeze through, then lowered himself down into the cavern. Jenny called to Caitlin that it was all right, but Caitlin shrieked anyway when Bone Heart picked her up.

Bone Heart carried Caitlin up to the crevice, put

his legs outside, then lifted her carefully out. Jenny looked away, rather than stare at the Indian's bare buttocks as he leaned through the opening.

"He didn't hurt you, did he?" Caitlin asked as her head emerged.

"Don't be afraid," Jenny said.

Caitlin groaned as Bone Heart carried her away from the rock and placed her on a patch of grass. Then he trotted up the hillside and gathered his clothes and his rifle.

"You are from the wagon," he said.

"And you are the scout for the soldiers?" Jenny asked, looking at the Henry rifle.

"You have fought well," Bone Heart said. He motioned with the rifle to the south, where the wagon was. "Your men have shown great courage. It is good."

"I suppose you are going to take us back to the soldiers," Jenny said.

"No," Bone Heart said. "I am tired. I am going home now."

He was already walking away.

21

Three Forks—where the Arkansas, Verdrigris, and Grand Rivers converged on the border between the Cherokee and Creek nations—had once been a bustling commercial stop, but like many of its sister communities along the Texas road, it now lay mostly in ashes.

Although the Union stronghold of Fort Gibson was only a few miles to the east, Three Forks was a no-man's-land of suspicion and mistrust, where federal troops seldom ventured except in force. Loyalties of every kind were questioned here: North or South, Creek or Cherokee, Ridge or Treaty faction.

Patrick Fenn hitched Raven outside the only business left in Three Forks, a little general store and tavern that had been only partially burned. The roof was gone and had been replaced by canvas, but even the canvas showed signs of having been scorched sometime in the recent past.

The Greenfeather brothers tied their horses alongside Raven and followed Patrick through the open doorframe. The store was empty except for the proprietor, a fat old man in a greasy apron, who watched from his perch on a stool at the end of the counter.

"What have you got to drink?" Patrick asked.

"No whiskey," the man said. "No wine. Choc beer."

"What's that?"

"Choctaw beer," Luke said. "The real thing isn't bad, but the stuff they sell around here is a fermented mess of snakeskins and fish guts and God knows what else. But it'll do if you're thirsty."

The fat man poured a glass from a dark brown bottle and placed it on the counter.

"Five cents," he said.

Patrick dug into his pocket and came up with a two-cent piece.

"Got anything cheaper?"

"Go ahead," the man said. "It ain't selling anyway."

Patrick took the glass, wiped the rim with his sleeve, and drank. The concoction only vaguely resembled beer.

"They didn't spare the fish," Patrick said as he put the glass down. "I would have preferred them to go a little heavier on the snakeskin."

The old man laughed.

"You've got a sense of humor, boy," he said. "I like that."

Patrick smiled congenially.

"How many times this town been burned?"

"Hell, I've lost count," the old man said. "Every time somebody gets a burr under his saddle about something, they strike a match. I'd move, but this store is all I've got, so I keep my opinions to myself."

Patrick tried another sip, but shook his head and pushed the glass away.

"Has an ambulance wagon been through here in the last few days?" he asked.

"What's it to you?" the old man asked.

"My wife and my family's in it."

"Well, I reckon there was one rolled through here three nights ago," the old man said, wiping his hands on his apron. "You're the second person to ask me about it. There was a bunch of Yankees here yesterday askin' about it. Wanted to know if they stopped, how many was with them, and whether they had said anything about where they were headed."

"And what did you tell them?" Patrick asked.

"Look here, son," the old man said. "You're asking a helluva lot of questions for a lousy two cents."

Langston Greenfeather took a silver dollar from his vest pocket and laid it on the counter. The old man did not take it, but eyed it longingly.

"I told the soldier captain that they stopped and a talkative fellow bought some medicine," the man said. "Said he had an injured girl in the wagon and asked me if I knew anything about doctoring. I took a look. She was a one-legged girl, and that one leg was busted, and she had some cracked ribs. It looked to me like the leg had been set right, but there was nothin' more they could do except make her comfortable until it healed."

"Who else was with them?"

"Let me see," the proprietor said. "Two other women, one looked like a half-breed. A couple of brats. Another man or two, but I can't remember."

Patrick nodded.

"Did you tell the soldiers anything else?"

"Nope."

"How many soldiers were there?"

The old man made a face.

Patrick put his hand over the silver coin.

"How many?"

"Six," he said. "That includes the captain. They carried repeating rifles. I figured they would head back to Fort Gibson, where Blunt is now, but instead they left south down the road."

"Thank you," Patrick said.

He released the coin and the old man snatched it up.

"Come on," he told the Greenfeathers. "We've got some hard riding to do"

"Just so we understand one another," the old man said as they walked away. "Don't expect me to lie if somebody comes around here askin' about you. Unless, of course, you want to pay a little extra."

Patrick stopped in the doorway.

The old man ducked behind the counter, expecting Patrick to draw his pistol.

"Old man," he said, "I don't care if you tell the devil himself we were here."

22

On the morning of the last day of November, the ambulance rumbled across the old Creek Nation toll bridge over the Elk River, although it had been a long while since tolls had been collected. Frank reined the team to a stop and surveyed the site where, less than five months before, most of the Indian Territory had fallen to the Union in the battle of Honey Springs.

"Cooper left two hundred Confederates dead or dying here," Sweeney said, "and the Yankees called it a battle. If it had been the other way around, they would have called it a massacre."

"How far is the Confederate line?" Jenny asked.

"Twenty miles or so," Sweeney said. "That is, if General Cooper hasn't given up his position along the Canadian. But I don't reckon things have changed much, because it's winter. The fighting won't start again until the spring."

"Then we should be there this afternoon," Jenny said.

"Things are pretty clear between here and there," Sweeney said. "After we hit the Canadian, it will be a clean shot to the Red River. There won't be no more trouble."

"Don't be too sure of that," Frank said.

"Can we rest here for a bit?" Jenny asked. "It's

a nice spot, and I can wash Annabel's diapers out. Caitlin's ribs are hurting her something awful, and the children are tired of being cooped up for so long."

"I would rather keep moving," Frank said.

"Are you still worried about that bastard Moonlight?" Sweeney asked. "We haven't seen any sign of him since we were in the Cherokee Nation. Surely he's given up and headed back north. I know *I* would have."

"All right," Frank said. "But just for a couple of hours. I want to cross the Canadian while it's still daylight so they don't shoot us coming across."

"Good," Sweeney said. "I can go on another little forage party and rustle us up something to eat."

"I don't think food is all you steal," Frank said.

"That hurts," Sweeney said. "Here we are, nearly brothers-in-law, and you're talking me down in front of the family. I'll make you a deal, Frank: if what I do bothers you so much, you don't have to eat anything I bring back."

Frank drove the wagon off the road and down to the river, where the team drank. Jenny spread a blanket on the ground beneath an ancient oak and Botkins carried Caitlin over to it, placing her back against the tree so that she could see the river.

The day was unseasonably warm, and when

Caitlin closed her eyes and felt the wind on her face, she could almost imagine it was spring.

Botkins went to the wagon and came back with his carpetbag.

"I'm almost finished," he said. From the bag he took the wooden leg that Patrick had started to fashion from the piece of broken axle while they were back in Missouri, and he laid it on the blanket beneath Caitlin's knee.

"Your leg will fit in this socket here, and be locked in place with straps," Botkins said. The wooden leg was a mirror image of Caitlin's left, down to the swell of the calf and the narrow ankle. "Look how the foot hinges. You'll be able to walk, ride a horse, do just about anything except run a footrace."

"If only this other leg would heal," Caitlin said.

"You're knitting up quite well," Botkins said, gently feeling the bones through the fabric of her dress. "How's your ribs?"

"They hurt worse than my leg," she said.

"They will, for a long while," Botkins said. "But they're just cracked; you didn't puncture anything inside. Excuse me for saying so, Caitie, but you're tough as an old boot."

"Just what a girl likes to hear."

"We could paint this leg flesh-colored," Botkins offered. "Why, a person would hardly know the difference, unless they knocked on them."

"Or we could paint the real one wood-colored to match," Caitlin said. "Botkins, I'll always know the difference."

"I'm sorry."

"Don't be," Caitlin said. "You did a wonderful job. It does look just like the real thing, and when I wear it I will always think of you and Patrick and that damned old ambulance."

Botkins looked away.

"Where do you suppose Patrick is?"

"I don't know," Caitlin said. "But he'll catch up with us."

"Trudy doesn't seem to think so," he said. "She's up there on the bridge right now, looking north. She says she doesn't want to go any farther without him. . . . Pardon me, but I'd better go help Frank take care of the team."

Caitlin grasped his hand.

"Botkins," she said, and pulled him toward her. She gave him a hug, her hand behind his head. "You'd better get out your shaving kit. You're starting to grow a little stubble, and we're not out of the Indian Nations yet."

Sweeney was back in an hour. He had two rabbits slung over his shoulder, and he knelt beside the river while he cleaned them. When he was finished he washed his hands and gave the meat to Trudy, who had already started a fire.

"The pickings were slim," Sweeney said as he

sat down on the blanket next to Caitlin. "Everything is clean as a cat hair for miles around."

"No purses to pinch?" Frank asked.

"Nary a one," Sweeney said. "I hate rabbit," he said, wiping his palms on his trousers. "You can never get that smell off your hands. It's supposed to be better this time of year, but it always stinks to me."

"I don't mind," Caitlin said. "Would you just shut up and hold me, Sweeney?"

He put his arm around her shoulders.

"I wish it were night," he whispered in her ear. "With the moon full and bright. And I wish your ribs were healed up good, because you don't know how randy you make me."

"Then I'm glad they're not," Caitlin said.

"Don't you trust me?"

"Not as far as I could throw you," she said. "I'm not saying that I don't have feelings for you, Thomas Jefferson Sweeney. Lord knows you make my stomach feel like it was turned inside out. But it just wouldn't be right."

"Why?" he asked. "Because I don't want to get hitched?"

"Because you're not going to stick around," she said. "We both know it, despite the games you're playing with Frank. Sweeney, you're the handsomest rascal I've ever known, and you've got more dash than a dozen ordinary fellows. You don't know how much I ache to give you what you want—what *I* want. But sooner or later you'd be gone. You can't stop chasing women any more than you can stop stealing."

"Wouldn't you regret not giving it to me?"

"Probably every day for the rest of my life," Caitlin said. "But it just wouldn't be right. That's just the way it is. The only thing I can't figure out is, why me?"

"I won't lie to you," he said. "I've been with a batch of pretty women all over—married, single, widowed, it's made no difference to me—and not a one can hold a candle to you. Not only are you pretty, you're smart, strong-willed, and determined. You know what needs to be done and you do it."

Caitlin shook her head.

"It's not going to work, Sweeney. I won't give in."

"I'm not trying to make you," he said. "You know, I just lied to you, right after I told you I wasn't. Not the part about you being pretty and smart, because that's so. The part about me being with a lot of women. It ain't true. I've never had a pretty girl in my life."

"Can't I believe a word you say?"

"The truth is, Cait, that I'm not worth your spit. I can't marry you because I'm not good enough for you."

"You're plenty good," Caitlin said. "You just try your best not to show it."

He shook his head.

"I haven't even told you my real name"

"I know. What is it?"

"Hubert," he said. "Hubert Hacklesford. It doesn't exactly roll off the tongue, does it?"

Caitlin giggled.

"I can't imagine a guerrilla named Hubert Hacklesford," she said. "But 'Thomas Jefferson Sweeney' has dash. I don't blame you; I would have changed my name, too."

"I made it up on the spot that first night we met," he said. "Just because I wanted to impress you. I never was a real guerrilla—I was a terrible coward, just a thief. Then I started feeling different because of the name, more confident, and then I started acting different. Suddenly I wasn't a coward anymore."

"Don't worry," she said. "I won't tell."

"You don't think it's dishonest?"

"No," she said. "Hubert Hacklesford is dead. Long live Thomas Jefferson Sweeney."

"I'm staying," Trudy said.

She was standing in the middle of the road on the south side of the toll bridge, her arms crossed, her feet planted. She refused to get inside the ambulance.

"Don't be foolish," Frank said.

"I'm going to wait right here," she said. "When he comes down this road, he's going to find me waiting for him. If he doesn't come, I'm going to die on this spot waiting for him. Either way, I'm not going another foot without Patrick."

"You don't have any food," Frank said. "There's no shelter. The weather is going to change and it will be damned cold in a few days. You'll freeze to death, if you don't starve first."

"Maybe so," Trudy said.

"Patrick would want you to come with us," Sweeney said. He was mounted on Splitfoot. The horse threw his head nervously and shuffled backward.

"Stop talking about him like he's already dead. I know he wants me to wait for him."

"Dammit," Frank said. "You're acting like a child."

"Why don't you come with us to the river?" Jenny suggested. "We will all wait on the north bank for Patrick. If he doesn't come in a day or two, and if you decide to stay, at least you'll be safer there."

Trudy hesitated.

"All right," she said finally. "But I won't cross the river without him."

23

The Canadian River shimmered with fire as the dying sun touched the horizon. The western sky was streaked with winter clouds the color of gunmetal, while in the east, stars were already beginning to shine.

The ambulance creaked to a stop on the sandy, sloping road that descended to the river. Botkins set the brake and gathered the reins while Frank jumped down from the seat. Sweeney, who was still riding Splitfoot, rode ahead a few yards and stood in the stirrups, inspecting the high bank on the opposite side of the river.

The water was wide but not too deep at the crossing. Trees covered both sides of the river, and closer down, willows trailed their tired-looking branches in the muddy water.

Halfway across the river was a small fieldpiece, a twelve-pound mountain howitzer, resting unevenly on its ruined carriage. The little cannon had become a white elephant of the border war, having changed hands half a dozen times and then abandoned each time when its new owners found it too cumbersome for a war fought largely on horseback. It had been abandoned for good when it had fallen from a packhorse and shattered a wheel during the retreat from Honey Springs.

A group of Confederate pickets lined the top of the opposite bank, looking like stick figures at this distance from the wagon. They had watched in alarm as the ambulance approached. Several of the pickets were waving their hats above their heads.

Sweeney returned the gesture.

"Maybe I'd better cross and parlay with them," Sweeney called back. "They seem awfully curious. Maybe they think we're touched, stopping on this side of the river."

Sweeney rode down to the river's edge and urged Splitfoot into the water, then stopped. The pickets were shouting something, but they were too far away for Sweeney to understand the words above the murmur of the water. But there was something disturbing in their manner; they were too animated. One of them raised his rifle in the air. Sweency saw the puff of smoke from the end of the barrel before he heard the report roll across the water.

"There's something wrong," Sweeney called, turning Splitfoot back toward the wagon. "Frank, load up—"

The trees on both sides of the road where the wagon stood quivered with fire and smoke.

A bullet struck Sweeney in the right shoulder, and he dropped from the saddle into the water. Splitfoot bolted down the bank, a burst of sand exploding from his hooves.

Botkins released the brake, took up the reins, and whipped the team as Frank shouted for the others to lie flat against the bed of the wagon. Frank pulled the Henry from behind the seat and fired wildly at the trees.

Six mounted soldiers burst from behind the trees, with Moonlight in the lead.

Sweeney stood, drew a pistol with his left hand, and staggered to a cottonwood log on the bank. He threw himself behind the log, his ears pricking to the thud of bullets pelting the other side.

"This is it," Frank said. "We can't make it."

"We'll make it," Botkins said. "Take your time and *aim.*"

Frank sucked in his breath, threw the rifle down on the soldier closing the gap on his side of the wagon, and fired. The trooper's rifle cartwheeled in the air as he fell backward over the rump of his horse.

Jenny lay beside Caitlin, with Little Frank and Annabel beneath them. The canvas above puckered as bullets passed through it. Trudy had drawn her pistol and was firing over the tailgate. She missed the first two soldiers she aimed at, but knocked the horse from beneath the third one. The trooper hit the ground near Sweeney, who promptly shot him through the heart.

The team reached the river and water plumed from the wheels of the wagon.

"I told you we'd make it," Botkins shouted.

Then he toppled from the seat amid a shower of blood and bone as a bullet struck the back of his bald head. Frank lunged for the reins, but they were carried beneath the wagon in Botkins's dead hands.

With the drag on the reins, the team veered sharply to the left. The ambulance went up on two wheels, and Frank was thrown off into the water. A terrific cracking sound followed as the tongue tore free. The horses continued, leaving the wagon behind. The trailing ends of the harness snagged in the carriage of the howitzer, and the little cannon was jerked down the river behind the team.

The ambulance righted itself, rolled a few more yards, and came to stop in knee-deep water.

Frank searched frantically for the rifle, but could not find it in the dark water. A soldier rode up and knocked Frank backward with the butt of his gun.

Frank lay back on his elbows in the water, watching the other end of the rifle now come to bear.

"Go to hell," Frank mumbled through his bloody mouth.

The soldier lowered the rifle.

"You first," he said.

There was a pistol shot and the soldier suddenly stiffened, clawing at the small of his back as if he had been stung by a bee. He fell slowly, landing face-first in the water.

Patrick was riding down the sloping bank, a revolver in each hand, the reins in his teeth. Behind him were the Greenfeathers, and all were firing as they came.

Trudy climbed over the tailgate, her now-empty revolver still clutched in her hand. She was calling Patrick's name as she waded through the river, oblivious to everything else around her.

At point-blank range, Moonlight shot her in the stomach.

"You bloody bastard," Sergeant O'Reilly said, and cracked Moonlight on the head with the barrel of his gun.

The sergeant then turned his horse and made a run for it with the two troopers who were left, but by now the pickets had made their way across the river and were waiting. Caught in a cross fire, all three fell dead before they reached the bank.

Trudy was on her knees in the water, her arms folded across her stomach. Her dress billowed around her and the river was stained reddish brown.

Patrick jumped from the saddle and ran to her. He lifted her from the water and carried her to the bank. He gently placed her down, then leaned over and brushed her lips with his.

She looked up and smiled.

"I didn't cross the river without you," she said.

After a few minutes Patrick got to his feet and waded back into the river toward the ambulance. The pickets had lifted Caitlin and the children out of the wagon and carried them to the far bank. Sweeney had followed, with Jenny's help.

Moonlight was sitting in the water, holding his head under the watchful eyes of Luke Greenfeather and his ever-present shotgun.

Frank was slumped against the tailgate.

"She's dead," Patrick said.

Frank tried to speak, but found that he had no words. He put his hand on Patrick's shoulder and squeezed, but Patrick brushed him aside.

Patrick drew a revolver. He inspected the cylinder. It had one live chamber left. He pressed the muzzle against Moonlight's temple and thumbed back the hammer.

"I ought to kill you right here," Patrick said. He lowered the revolver. "But I can't. If I do, that makes me no better than you are."

Patrick turned away. He rubbed his eyes with his hands, then looked back toward the bank where Trudy lay.

"'Give me his gage,'" Moonlight said dreamily. Blood ran from the gash in his forehead down his face. "'Lions make leopards tame.'"

Patrick lifted the revolver.

"Like hell I can't."

Epilogue

Winter Camp
Mineral Creek, Texas
December 1863

The young guerrilla chieftain stood in front of the window, his hands clasped behind his back, and gazed with lazy blue eyes through the cracked panes at the hard-packed Texas street.

Behind him on the writing desk was a half-finished letter to General Sterling Price, one that he had attempted to write a dozen times before. Beside his abandoned pen was a sword.

His reverie was broken when a battered Union ambulance wagon rolled to a stop in the middle of the street. It resembled the ambulance that had been liberated from Blunt's command following the victory at Baxter Springs a few weeks earlier, but it couldn't be the same one, the guerrilla leader reasoned; that vehicle had been new, with a gleaming coat of fresh paint.

A gaunt young man was driving the ambulance, and on the seat beside him was a woman with a little boy on her lap. Abreast of the ambulance rode a younger man on a big black horse, a brace of revolving pistols at his belt. The two men bore a striking resemblance and were obviously brothers.

A third man jumped lightly from the tailgate of the ambulance and helped a red-haired young woman to the ground. One of the woman's legs was in a heavy wooden splint, and she moved slowly, as if more than her limbs had been battered. In her arms was a baby.

The family talked for some time with the grim young man on the black horse. He spoke little. Finally he shook his head and, without looking back, turned the magnificent horse and rode slowly back to the north.

The guerrilla leader had seen the look in the young man's face before, on the faces of his young lieutenants: it was the hopeless, hard-set look of revenge.

He turned away from the scene and resumed his seat at the desk. He stared at the unfinished letter for a moment, refilled his pen with ink, and continued.

> . . . I trust this sets straight any mis-
> understandings that may have reached
> you, sir, of the particulars of my campaign
> along the Missouri and Kansas rivers,
> and especially of the incidents concerning
> the destruction of the city of Lawrence. I
> now have gathered with me at my winter
> camp some three hundred and fifty of
> that daring and dashing character of men
> that made the summer's campaign so

successful, and I look forward to pressing them into the service of the noble struggle come spring.

It has been my modest desire in relating these events to you that the murderous and inhuman character of our enemy may be accurately portrayed to the Confederacy and, indeed, to the world.

I have the honor to remain, respectfully, your obedient servant,

Wm. C. Quantrill
Colonel, CSA

The young leader studied the finished letter for a long while.

Then he snatched it from the desk and crumpled it into a tight ball.

ABOUT THE AUTHOR

Max McCoy is an award-winning journalist and native Kansan. His first novel, *The Sixth Rider*, won the Medicine Pipe Bearer's Award for the best first novel in 1991 from the Western Writers of America. *Home to Texas* is his fifth novel.

Center Point Large Print
600 Brooks Road / PO Box 1
Thorndike, ME 04986-0001 USA

(207) 568-3717

US & Canada:
1 800 929-9108
www.centerpointlargeprint.com